Veins of Vengance

The Notturno Affair, Volume 2

R. Stellan

Published by R. Stellan, 2024.

This is a work of fiction. Similarities to real people, places, or events are entirely coincidental.

VEINS OF VENGANCE

First edition. November 21, 2024.

Copyright © 2024 R. Stellan.

ISBN: 979-8227538901

Written by R. Stellan.

Table of Contents

Shadows of the Past 1
Unlikely Allies 11
A Bitter Betrayal 22
Tides of Vengeance 36
Secrets in the Dark 49
Heart of the Storm 66
The Longest Night 79
Into the Fire 93
Blood and Bond 109
Echoes of Betrayal 121
The Silent War 130
Crossroads 142
The Price of Freedom 153
Next in the series! 165

Dedication

To my family, whose love and unwavering support have been the foundation of my strength. To those who fight not just for survival, but for justice, redemption, and the chance to reclaim their destiny. And to every reader who dares to face their darkest fears, knowing that hope can always rise from the ashes.

May this story remind you that vengeance can be a path to healing, and that even in the deepest shadows, there's always a chance for light.

"Vengeance is not a path to peace, but the key that unlocks the door to the truth we dare not face."

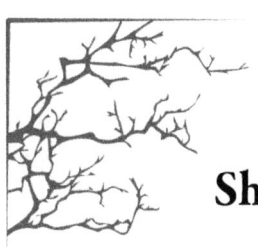

Shadows of the Past

The sun was setting behind the hills, casting long shadows across the estate, and for a moment, it almost felt like everything was at peace. Almost. Ruby and I were walking through the Rose Garden, her hand warm in mine as we talked about our plans for the week. I should've felt grateful—hell, I *was* grateful—but something gnawed at me from the inside. It had been a year since I'd heard anything from the people I'd left behind, from the world I'd tried to bury. But silence was never a good sign in my past. It was only a matter of time before they came knocking, and I knew, deep down, that whatever came next would threaten everything I'd built with Ruby.

"Ryan, what's wrong?" Ruby's voice broke through my thoughts. Her eyes, always so perceptive, locked onto mine with concern. "You've been quiet all evening."

I tried to smile, brushing a stray lock of her chestnut hair behind her ear. "Nothing. Just thinking about some things."

"Thinking about *what*?" she asked, her voice gentle but insistent.

I paused. This was the moment. The moment I had been dreading, but had always known would come. I had told her everything I could—everything she needed to know—but there were pieces of my past that I had kept hidden from her. Not because I didn't trust her, but because I wanted to protect her from the darkness I had once lived in.

But how long could I keep her in the dark? How long could I shield her from the truth of the life I'd left behind? Before I could answer, a figure appeared at the edge of the garden. My heart skipped a beat, recognizing the silhouette even before he stepped fully into the light. It was Leo. His face was grim, his eyes scanning the estate with a vigilance that made my stomach twist. He was always the one who kept an eye on things, but the way he looked at me now told me something was wrong.

"Ryan," he called, his tone low, "we need to talk."

Ruby squeezed my hand, sensing the shift in the air. "What's going on?" she asked, her voice tense now. I didn't want to pull her into it—not yet, not when she was finally starting to feel safe again. But Leo's presence alone was enough to make my past feel like it was coming for us. The questions she had, the suspicions, I could see them starting to form behind her eyes.

"I don't know," I said quietly. "But it looks like the past has a way of catching up with me."

Ruby's grip tightened around my hand, and I could see the determination in her eyes. "We face things together, Ryan. You don't have to go through this alone." I wanted to tell her that I was trying to protect her from this life, from the shadows I could never fully outrun. But I knew, as much as I wanted to shield her, I couldn't hide the truth forever. The danger was coming, and it wouldn't be long before it knocked on our door.

"Let's go inside," I said, leading her towards the mansion.

Leo fell in step beside us, his presence a silent reminder of the storm that was brewing.

We entered the house, and I led Ruby into the study, closing the door behind us. "What's going on, Leo?" I asked, trying to keep my voice steady. Leo stood by the window, watching the darkening sky, his jaw clenched.

"I don't know the details yet, but there are whispers. People from your past. They're looking for you, Ryan. And they don't care who they hurt to find you." My heart sank, and Ruby's face fell as she glanced between us. "Who? Who's after you?" I sighed, running a hand through my hair. "It's the people I left behind. The family I walked away from. My father's organization. I thought I'd gotten away from them, but it looks like I was wrong." Ruby's eyes softened, and she reached out to touch my arm. "You don't have to face this alone. We'll figure it out together." I met her gaze, her unwavering support both a comfort and a burden. The weight of what was coming hit me all at once—Ruby was my everything. She had been my light in the darkest times. But could I really drag her into the darkness that had always been a part of me? Could I risk her safety to keep her by my side?

Leo cleared his throat, drawing my attention back to him. "I've been keeping an eye on things. They're getting closer, Ryan. And they won't stop until they get what they want."

"What do they want?" Ruby asked, her voice steady despite the fear creeping into her eyes.

I took a deep breath. "Me. And they won't stop until I'm either dead or back in the fold. My family's business doesn't just let people walk away."

The silence that followed was heavy, the weight of my words settling between us. Ruby took a step closer, standing beside me, her presence a silent promise that we'd face whatever was coming together.

"I'm not going anywhere," she said, her voice firm. "We'll fight this. Together."

I wanted to believe that. But I couldn't help the nagging fear that the darkness of my past might be too much for us to outrun. The fire crackled in the hearth, its glow casting a warm light over the study, but the chill in the air around us felt far deeper than the cool night creeping through the windows. I looked at Ruby, her face set with determination, and then back at Leo, who remained near the window, watching the horizon as though he could see the danger approaching.

"What now?" I asked, my voice rough, though I knew the answer. We couldn't outrun this. Not anymore.

Leo turned from the window, his eyes steady. "I've been in touch with some old contacts. They say there's been movement—talk of a power shift in the organization. Your father's death has triggered chaos, and now others are scrambling for control. They're looking for a new leader, someone to step in and bring order back to the family." I felt my chest tighten at the mention of my father. His death hadn't been a loss; but it had been a violent end to a violent life. Shot by my mother, Judie, in an act of self-defence, it had unravelled everything—our family, our lives, the very foundation of the empire he'd built. But his death hadn't ended the danger. It only complicated everything. My father might be gone, but the shadows of his empire stretched far beyond the grave.

"They're still out there, aren't they?" I muttered, more to myself than to Leo.

Leo's expression hardened, and he nodded slowly. "The Giovannetti family isn't just about your father. It's a network of power that won't simply disappear. And with your father gone, the vacuum he left is being fought over. The question is—who do they think will take control now?" My stomach churned at the thought. The idea that anyone would consider me a candidate for leadership in the *Famiglia Notturno* was a sickening one. I had no interest in returning to that life. No matter how much blood ran through my veins, I wasn't that person anymore.

"I left that life behind," I said, my voice low. "I've made it clear. I've made my choice. I'm not going back to that world. No one gets to decide that for me."

Ruby stepped forward, her hand on my arm, grounding me. "But they're still going to try, aren't they?" I nodded. "They will." I could feel the weight of her gaze, full of concern, but also of strength. Ruby knew me better than anyone. She knew I'd never be able to fully escape the consequences of my past, no matter how hard I tried. "If it's not the old guard, it'll be someone else trying to fill the void."

"And they'll come after us," she said, voice tight with resolve. "After you. After us."

The thought of Ruby being dragged into the chaos again sent a ripple of anger through me. The last thing I wanted was to bring her back into this.

"What's our move, Ryan?" Leo asked, breaking my thoughts.

I took a deep breath, staring out the window into the darkness. I could hear the hum of the estate's security systems in the background, a constant reminder that we were trying to keep something out... or, more likely, trying to keep us in.

"I need to know who's behind this," I said, my tone sharp. "Who's trying to make a move. We can't let this drag us back into their mess."

Ruby's hand tightened on mine, and I felt her unease. "Ryan, whatever happens... we face it together. I won't let you go through this alone."

"I never wanted this for you," I said, my voice thick with emotion. "You shouldn't have to fight this war."

Ruby smiled softly, but there was no hesitation in her eyes. "It's not just your war, Ryan. It's ours." Leo cleared his throat. "I'll reach out to a few trusted people who can help us. But this is going to take time. We need to stay vigilant. The moment we let our guard down, that's when they'll strike." Ruby's gaze met mine, and for a long moment, the world seemed to shrink to just the two of us. The weight of what was coming, the darkness of the past resurfacing, didn't seem so insurmountable with her by my side. And for that, I was more grateful than words could express.

"I'm not going to let you down," I whispered.

She squeezed my hand. "And I'll never let you go." The sound of the grandfather clock ticking in the corner seemed louder now, marking the passage of time that felt both endless and unbearably quick. The air between us was heavy with the weight of unspoken thoughts and fears. My mind kept racing back to the news Leo had given us—movement in the organization. The empire I had tried so desperately to distance myself from, the one I had hoped would fade into history with my father's death, was stirring again. And with it, the threats. The danger. The price of my past.

"Ryan, we need a plan," Ruby's voice cut through my thoughts, soft but firm.

I met her gaze, the same resolve in her eyes that had always been there, even when the odds were stacked against us. I couldn't help but feel a rush of gratitude and frustration. Grateful for her unwavering support, but frustrated that I couldn't protect her from the storm that was coming. This wasn't the life I'd wanted for her, for us. But as always, she was right there beside me, ready to face whatever came next.

"I know," I said, running a hand through my hair. "I just... I can't keep going back to that world. I can't let it drag you into it again."

Ruby stepped closer, her voice softening. "You don't have to do it alone. We're a team, Ryan. We've always been a team." Leo shifted in the background, his expression serious. "We'll need to keep a low profile for now. No one can know we're making any moves. But that won't stop them. Whoever is trying to take over will come looking for us. They'll want to test you, Ryan." I leaned back against the desk, my mind trying to focus. "And if they do? What then?" Ruby placed a hand on my shoulder, her touch grounding me. "Then we face it head-on. Together. You don't have to carry this alone." Her words struck me deeply. How many times had I thought I had to carry everything by myself? How many times had I tried to push her away for fear of dragging her into my mess? And yet, here she was—by my side, ready to face the darkness that I had run from for so long.

I shook my head, the burden feeling heavier with every passing moment. "I don't want you caught in the crossfire. I won't let them hurt you."

"Ryan," Ruby said, her voice soft yet resolute. "You can't shield me from everything. I don't need you to protect me. I just need you to trust me. Trust us."

A silent beat passed between us, her words sinking deep into my chest. Trust. It had always been the hardest thing for me. Trust in myself, in the world around me. But with Ruby, I'd learned to trust in something greater. Us. Our love, our strength.

"Okay," I said finally, my voice steady. "I trust you. I trust us."

Leo cleared his throat again, drawing our attention back to the matter at hand. "We need to move fast. I'll make the calls, set up meetings with the people who might be able to help us find out who's pulling the strings now. But this is going to get messy. We'll need to be ready for anything." Ruby nodded. "We will be." I stood up, pacing for a moment, then turned back to them both. "I'm not going back to that life. But we're not just going to wait for them to come knocking. We take control. We stop this before it gets out of hand."

"Agreed," Leo said, his voice low but firm. "We fight back."

The three of us shared a moment of understanding. The fight ahead wouldn't be easy, but we had no choice. Our future was on the line. The ghosts of my past were circling, but I wouldn't let them take us down. Not now. Not ever. As the conversation drifted into more tactical plans, my mind kept returning to the same thought—whatever was coming, we would face it together. Ruby, Leo, Mia—our people, our family. We'd been through hell and back before, and we'd make it through again. But the silence on the other side of the estate, the hum of the security systems, felt like a countdown to something inevitable. A storm was coming. And I had no choice but to brace for it. The fire in the hearth flickered, casting long shadows across the study as I sat down at the desk, my thoughts swirling with the decisions ahead. Ruby and Leo were still standing nearby, their presence a constant reminder that we weren't in this alone. But even with them here, I couldn't shake the feeling of impending danger that hung in the air like a storm cloud. The past was clawing its way back, and no matter how far I'd run, it was coming for me again. Leo spoke first, breaking the silence. "We need to think about how they'll approach us. If someone's trying to step into your father's role, they'll want to establish power quickly. That means they'll test you, Ryan. They'll push." I nodded grimly. Leo was right. They wouldn't waste time. They'd come after me, test my loyalty, my resolve—see if I was still the same man who had been groomed to take over the family business, the same man who had once ruled the shadows of the underworld. But that man was dead. I was no longer that person.

"Let them come," I said, my voice colder than I intended. "We won't play by their rules. I'm not getting dragged into this again."

Ruby placed a hand on my arm, grounding me, her touch a reminder that I wasn't alone in this fight. "We'll do this on our terms, Ryan. But we need to be careful. The people who are trying to take control—they know you. They'll know how to push your buttons." I looked at her, seeing the concern etched in her eyes. "I won't let them pull us into this. Not again."

"I know," she said softly, her thumb brushing over my hand. "But we have to stay vigilant. The last thing we want is to be caught off guard."

Leo moved towards the door, turning back to face us. "I'll keep in touch with the contacts. We need information. We need to know who's making moves in the dark. The more we know, the better we can plan."

I stood up, walking over to the window, my gaze lingering on the darkened estate grounds outside. The night was still, but it felt like the calm before a storm. I couldn't ignore the gnawing feeling that things were about to get worse.

"Ryan," Ruby said, her voice soft but firm. "You're not alone in this. We'll face whatever comes together. You've got me, you've got Leo, you've got Mia. We're in this as a family."

I turned to her, my heart tightening. There was no one I trusted more than Ruby. But that didn't change the fact that her safety was my top priority. If it came down to it, I'd risk everything to protect her.

"I just want you safe," I said quietly, stepping toward her. "I'll do whatever it takes to keep you out of harm's way."

Ruby reached up, cupping my face in her hands. "You don't need to protect me, Ryan. We protect each other. Always." Her words brought a fierce sense of clarity. I'd spent too long trying to shield her from the world I'd been born into. But the truth was, she had always been my equal, my partner in every sense of the word. I couldn't hide behind my fears anymore.

"We'll handle it," I said, my voice more certain now. "Together."

There was a long silence as I gazed at Ruby, the weight of what was coming pressing down on both of us. I knew what we were facing wouldn't be easy. I knew the danger would escalate, and the stakes were higher than they'd ever been. But for the first time in a long while, I wasn't afraid. With Ruby by my side, we could face anything. And yet, a part of me couldn't shake the nagging thought that we hadn't seen the worst of it yet.

"Leo," I said, my voice steady, "keep your ear to the ground.

We need to know exactly who's making a move and why. I don't care if it's the old guard or someone new. We need answers." Leo nodded, his face grim. "I'll get to work. Stay sharp, both of you." As he left the room, I turned back to Ruby, the weight of the coming battle settling over me. The family legacy—the empire my father had built—wasn't just a past I could bury. It was alive, pulsing through my veins, and no matter how hard I tried to escape it, it would always find a way to drag me back. But I wouldn't let it break me. Not now. Not with Ruby by my side.

"I'm not going back to that world, Ruby," I said, my voice low but resolute. "But we're not running either. We'll face this head-on. Together."

She smiled, her eyes steady, filled with a quiet strength that always anchored me. "We always have, Ryan. And we always will." The door to the study clicked closed behind Leo, and I stood there for a moment, my hand resting on Ruby's. Outside, the wind picked up, the trees rustling in the distance. The storm was coming. And this time, we were ready to face it.

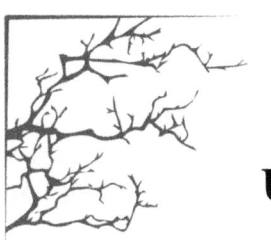

Unlikely Allies

The estate felt quieter than usual, as if the very walls were holding their breath, waiting for something to happen. The days since Leo had left to gather more information had passed in a blur of half-formed plans and restless nights. Ruby and I had barely slept, our minds consumed with what could be coming next. I stood in front of the window, staring out over the estate's sprawling gardens, though my thoughts were far from the serenity outside. Leo's contacts hadn't come through with much. Information in the criminal world was hard to come by, especially when the people you were dealing with liked to keep their cards close. But I could feel it—there was something big on the horizon, and we weren't prepared for it.

"Ryan?" Ruby's voice broke through my thoughts.

She stood in the doorway, her expression soft but her eyes sharp, as always. She knew when something was off with me. I turned to face her, meeting her gaze. "I'm just thinking. Trying to figure out our next move." Her lips pressed into a line, her brow furrowed. "You're still pushing yourself too hard. You don't have to do this alone." I crossed the room toward her, taking her hands in mine. "It's not about doing it alone. It's about making sure you're safe. The last thing I want is for this mess to pull you back into a world you left behind." Ruby tilted her head, her eyes filled with understanding. "You've never had to protect me, Ryan. We've always faced things together."

Her words were a reminder of why I loved her—because she never backed down, never let me carry the weight alone. She was my equal in every way. But that didn't change the fact that the threats we were facing now were bigger, more dangerous than anything I'd ever faced. And no matter how much I wanted to shield her from it, I couldn't.

"I know," I said quietly. "But this... this feels different."

Before she could respond, the door to the study opened, and Leo stepped inside, his face tense. "Ryan, Ruby... we need to talk." My stomach dropped. Leo's tone had the weight of something serious behind it.

> "What is it?" I asked, my mind already running through the possibilities.

> "It's about an old contact of yours. Someone from your father's past," Leo said, his voice laced with unease. "I didn't expect this, but... we may need their help."

I frowned. "Help? Who the hell could we possibly trust from that side of things?" Leo hesitated, clearly not comfortable with what he was about to say. "Giovanni Mancini." I felt my chest tighten at the mention of the name. Giovanni Mancini was a name I never thought I'd hear again. He was a part of my father's network, a ruthless businessman with connections that ran deep in the underworld. We'd crossed paths more than once in my younger years, but that had been before I left it all behind.

> "Giovanni?" Ruby's voice was incredulous, and I knew exactly how she felt. "The Mancini family was always in bed with your father's empire. Why would you even consider working with him?"

I ran a hand through my hair, feeling the weight of the decision bearing down on me. "I know. Believe me, I know. But we don't have the luxury of being picky right now. Giovanni's connections run deep, and if we're going to survive what's coming, we need information. We need to know who's making moves and how to strike first." Ruby was silent for a moment, clearly processing the situation. "And you think Giovanni will help us?"

"He won't do anything for free," I replied, my voice tinged with bitterness. "But he may be our only option."

Leo stepped forward, crossing his arms. "I've already made contact. He's expecting us." I felt a knot form in my stomach. This was the last thing I wanted. Giovanni Mancini was as dangerous as they come, and he didn't do favours without a price. But I couldn't be picky. If working with him was the only way to protect Ruby and the estate, then I'd have to swallow my pride.

"Fine," I said, my voice firm. "We'll meet him. But we do this on our terms. If he tries to pull anything..."

"I'll take care of it," Leo said, his tone steady. "I won't let him screw us over."

Ruby stepped closer to me, her eyes searching my face. "Are you sure about this, Ryan?" I met her gaze, my heart heavy. "No. But we don't have a choice."

Later that evening, the three of us made our way to the meeting location—an old, abandoned warehouse on the outskirts of the city. It was a place that had seen its share of deals, both legitimate and not-so-legitimate. Giovanni's signature touch was evident—the place was secure, heavily guarded, with armed men at every entrance. I could feel Ruby's tension beside me, her hand firmly gripping mine as we walked toward the entrance. "Just stay close," I whispered, my voice low. She gave me a tight nod, her eyes scanning the area, ever watchful. Leo led the way, his demeanour calm, collected. He knew this world, knew the games being played. But even he couldn't mask the unease in the air as we approached the building. Giovanni Mancini wasn't someone you ever felt comfortable around. And tonight, I wasn't sure whether this meeting was going to be a lifeline—or a death sentence. As we entered the warehouse, the air grew thick with tension. At the far end of the room, behind a large oak desk, Giovanni sat waiting. He was older than I remembered, his once-dark hair now streaked with grey, his sharp features hardened by years of power and betrayal. He gave us a small, knowing smile as we approached.

"Ryan Giovannetti," Giovanni said, his voice smooth and calculated. "It's been a long time."

I felt the bitterness rise in my chest at the sound of my father's name on his lips. But I pushed it down, focusing on the task at hand.
"Let's get this over with," I said, my tone cold.

Giovanni's smile widened, though there was no warmth in it. "I'm glad to see you've learned to get to the point. So, what exactly is it you need from me?"

I met his gaze, my resolve hardening. "Information. About the people who are trying to take control of the family. The ones making moves in the shadows. We need to know who they are."
Giovanni leaned back in his chair, studying us for a moment before nodding. "I can give you that. But everything comes at a price, Ryan. You know that better than anyone." I had expected as much. But I wasn't about to make a deal with Giovanni without knowing the cost.

"Just tell us what you want," I said. "We'll decide if it's worth it."

Giovanni chuckled, his eyes gleaming with amusement. "Of course you'll decide. But don't take too long. Time is always of the essence in this business." And with that, the game began. The silence between us was thick as Giovanni studied us, his eyes flicking between Ruby, Leo, and me, as though weighing the very air in the room. The tension was palpable, the kind that could snap at any moment.

"I'm not interested in your games, Giovanni," I said, my voice steady, but the edge of anger underlying my words was clear. "You don't get to play with us anymore. Not like you did with my father."

Giovanni's lips curled into a thin, amused smile. He leaned forward in his chair, steepling his fingers, his eyes never leaving mine. "Your father's mistakes are not mine to explain, Ryan. I merely adapted to the world we lived in. But you know this world. It's in your blood. That's why we're talking now." Ruby's hand tightened around mine, and I felt her unease ripple through her. She wasn't blind to the danger that lay in these conversations, and I wasn't either. But I couldn't afford to show weakness—not now, not when we were this close to finding answers.

"Cut to the chase," Leo said, his voice low, but with a quiet authority that Giovanni respected. "We're not here to talk about the past. We're here for information. What do you know about the people trying to take control?"

Giovanni gave a slow, deliberate nod, clearly enjoying the tension in the room. "Patience, Leo. All in due time." He leaned back again, assessing us as though savouring the moment. "But since you've asked... I know a lot. I always do." I didn't like how he said that. Giovanni Mancini was one of those men who always had his fingers in more pies than you could count. He wasn't just well-connected; he was practically omnipresent in the shadows of the world I had tried to escape.

"Go on," I said, my tone pushing him. I needed to know, and I needed to know fast.

"There are several factions trying to seize power," Giovanni continued, his voice soft but calculated. "Some are old blood, like your family. They've been waiting for an opening for years. Others... they're more recent, hungry for power and willing to do whatever it takes to claim it. They don't care about family loyalties or tradition. They're in it for themselves."

I could feel the knot in my stomach tighten. These were the people I had been trying to avoid—the very reason I left that life behind. They were the predators, circling around the carcass of my father's empire, waiting for the right moment to strike.

"Who?" I pressed, unable to mask the urgency in my voice.
"Who's behind it? Who's pulling the strings?"

Giovanni's smile faded slightly, his eyes narrowing. "Patience, Ryan. I can tell you about them, but you need to understand the cost." He shifted, leaning forward, his gaze fixed on me. "Your father's death caused a ripple. And like all ripples, it's spreading. But what you need to understand is this: you can't fight this war with just information. You need allies. Real ones. Not just men with power or connections. You need people who owe you something. People who trust you."

Ruby's grip on my hand tightened, and I felt her steady presence beside me. "We don't need your games, Giovanni," she said, her voice sharp.

"We need your help, not your empty promises."

Giovanni's gaze flicked to her, his interest piqued. "Ah, the lovely Ruby. A woman of strength and conviction. It's rare to see someone with a backbone in this business anymore." I clenched my jaw, trying to keep my focus. "Just tell us who we need to watch out for, Giovanni. What's the price for the information?" Giovanni didn't answer right away. Instead, he motioned to a nearby table, where a bottle of aged whiskey sat, gleaming in the low light. "A drink, perhaps? It's always better to make a deal with a clear head."

"I'm not here to drink," I snapped. "I'm here for answers."

He raised an eyebrow, then leaned back in his chair again, eyes glittering with amusement. "Very well, Ryan. You've always been a man of business, not pleasure. I respect that." He paused, then spoke again, his voice darker this time. "You need to watch out for two players: Alessandro Vitale and Francesca D'Alessandro." The names hit me like a punch to the gut. Alessandro Vitale and Francesca D'Alessandro were two of the most dangerous people in the business. Vitale was a master of manipulation, always playing both sides of every deal, while Francesca was known for her ruthlessness—cold, calculating, and always willing to do whatever it took to secure her position.

> "Vitale and D'Alessandro?" I asked, barely able to keep the disbelief from my voice. "You're telling me they're involved in this?"

Giovanni's lips twisted into a tight smile. "I wouldn't be wasting your time if I wasn't sure. They're already making moves, trying to carve out their territory, taking advantage of the power vacuum your father left. And they're not alone. There are others working with them—people from within your father's old network." I felt a cold rage coil inside me. These were the very people I'd fought to escape. The very people who'd taken everything from me—my family, my peace, my future. And now they were back, coming for everything I'd fought to protect.

> "So, what do you want in return for this information?" I asked, my voice low and controlled.

Giovanni leaned forward again, his eyes gleaming. "I want a seat at the table, Ryan. When the dust settles, I want to be there, beside you. Not as an enemy, but as an ally. And if you want my help, you'll need to owe me. My name, my connections, they don't come for free." I stared at him, my mind racing. I'd known this would come, Giovanni never did anything without securing something for himself. But this was more than just an alliance. This was a bargain. And I wasn't sure if I could trust him.

"You want me to trust you?" I asked, my voice tight with disbelief. "You want me to make a deal with you after everything you've done?"

Giovanni's smile didn't waver. "Trust is a luxury, Ryan. But sometimes, it's a necessity. You can't afford to make this fight about pride. You need allies. You need power. And I can give you both." I looked over at Ruby, who met my gaze with a mix of concern and resolve. I could see the question in her eyes—should we make this deal? Could we trust Giovanni?

I turned back to Giovanni, my mind made up. "We'll consider it. But understand this—if you try to pull anything, I'll make sure you regret it."

Giovanni's smile widened, but there was something cold in his eyes. "I wouldn't expect anything less, Ryan. After all, we're both survivors, aren't we?" The meeting ended with Giovanni's departure, his words lingering like smoke in the room. I watched as his car disappeared into the darkness, taillights glowing like embers before they were swallowed by the night. The weight of his proposition hung heavy in the air, and for a moment, none of us spoke. Ruby broke the silence first. "Do you trust him?" I turned to her, meeting her steady gaze. "No," I admitted. "But we don't have much of a choice. If what he's saying about Vitale and D'Alessandro is true, we need every advantage we can get. Even if it means working with Giovanni." Leo crossed his arms, leaning back against the edge of the desk. "He's not lying about them. I've heard whispers about Vitale making moves, and Francesca... well, she's always been a wild card. But the fact that they're working together?" He shook his head. "That's dangerous. They don't just want power—they want control. Over everything."

"And they'll come after us to get it," Ruby said, her voice steady but laced with determination. "They won't stop until they have what they want."

I nodded, the tension in my chest tightening. "Which means we have to move first. We can't just wait for them to come to us." Leo raised an eyebrow. "And what does that look like? Because if you're thinking about charging headfirst into their territory, I'll tell you right now—it's a suicide mission."

"I'm not charging into anything," I said sharply. "But we need to find out what they're planning, who their allies are, and what their weaknesses are. Giovanni's information is a start, but it's not enough. We need more."

Ruby stepped closer to me, her hand brushing against mine. "Then we start with the contacts we trust. Leo, do you still have connections in Vitale's circles?" Leo nodded reluctantly. "A few. But reaching out to them is risky. If Vitale catches wind that I'm sniffing around, it could blow back on all of us."

"It's a risk we have to take," I said. "Start with the people you trust the most. Discreetly. We need to know what we're up against."

Leo gave a curt nod, his jaw tight. "I'll make some calls. But Ryan, you'd better be sure about this. Once we start digging, there's no going back." I turned back to Ruby, her eyes searching mine. "What about you?" she asked softly. "What's your next move?"

"I need to reach out to someone else," I said, my voice low. "Someone who might have more insight into what Vitale and Francesca are doing."

Ruby frowned. "Who?" I hesitated, the name caught in my throat. It was someone I hadn't spoken to in years, someone whose loyalty had always been... complicated. But if anyone had information, it was her.

"Clara," I said finally.

Ruby's expression hardened slightly. "Clara," she repeated.

"She worked with my father," I explained. "She was one of his top strategists, but she was always more interested in self-preservation than loyalty. If anyone knows what Vitale and Francesca are planning, it's her."

Ruby's jaw tightened, and I could see the flicker of unease in her eyes. "And you think she'll help us?"

"She might," I said. "If we give her the right incentive."

Leo let out a low whistle. "You're really reaching deep into the barrel for this one, Ryan. Clara's dangerous."

"She's also our best shot at getting ahead of this," I said firmly. "I'll handle her. Alone."

Ruby stepped closer, her hand gripping my arm. "No. We're in this together, remember? I'm not letting you face her alone."

"Ruby, Clara's..." I trailed off, searching for the right words. "She's not like Giovanni. She doesn't play games. She's calculated, and she'll exploit any weakness she sees. If you come with me—"

"I'm not a weakness, Ryan," Ruby interrupted, her voice steady and unyielding. "I'm your partner. And if you think

I'm just going to sit back while you walk into a meeting with someone like her, then you don't know me at all."

Her words hit me like a hammer, and I felt a rush of both frustration and admiration. Ruby was right. She wasn't a weakness—she was my strength. And I couldn't afford to underestimate her.

"Fine," I said finally. "We'll go together. But we do this my way. No unnecessary risks."

Ruby nodded, her determination unwavering. "Agreed." Leo let out a low chuckle. "Well, this should be interesting. Just don't forget—Clara's loyalty is to herself. Don't expect her to stick her neck out for you unless she sees something in it for her."

"I know," I said. "But we don't have much of a choice."

The room fell into a heavy silence again, the weight of the decisions we were making settling over us like a dark cloud. I glanced out the window, the distant lights of the estate barely visible against the encroaching darkness. The shadows of my past were closing in, and the fight ahead was going to be unlike anything we'd faced before. But as I looked at Ruby and Leo, I felt a flicker of resolve. Whatever came next, we'd face it together.

"Let's get to work," I said, my voice firm.

Because the war wasn't just coming—it had already begun.

A Bitter Betrayal

The storm outside mirrored the tension within the estate, rain lashing against the windows as thunder rumbled in the distance. I stood in the library, staring at the crackling fire but feeling no warmth from it. Ruby was seated on the edge of the couch, her hands gripping the armrest tightly, her jaw clenched as if she were holding back words. Leo paced in front of us, his usual calm demeanour replaced with an agitation I rarely saw. "You know what this means, don't you? Someone on the inside has been feeding them information. Vitale and Francesca couldn't have made that move without knowing exactly where to strike." Ruby glanced at me, her eyes sharp with concern. "Someone close to us."

I felt the words like a blow. The idea that someone within our circle—someone we trusted—had betrayed us was almost too much to comprehend. "We've kept this place locked down. Every move we've made, every precaution we've taken—it's all been airtight," I said, my voice low and tense. "There's no way they could've gotten in without help." Leo stopped pacing and turned to face me, his expression grim. "Ryan, we need to start asking some hard questions. Everyone in this house needs to be accounted for. No exceptions." Ruby straightened, her voice firm. "We can't start accusing people without proof, Leo. If we start tearing each other apart, we're doing exactly what they want." I nodded in agreement but felt a knot tightening in my stomach. "She's right. But we can't ignore the possibility that someone's turned against us. We need to handle this carefully—find out who's behind it without tipping our hand."

Leo exhaled sharply. "Fine. But if we don't figure this out fast, we're sitting ducks. They already got too close this time. Next time, they might not miss." Ruby looked at me, her hand reaching for mine. "We'll figure this out. Together." Her touch grounded me, and I nodded, though the weight of the situation bore down heavily. "We will," I said, my voice steadier than I felt. "But first, we need to figure out who had access to the plans for the shipment. That's where the leak is." Leo's eyes narrowed, his mind already working through the possibilities. "I'll start with the staff. Quietly. If anyone's been acting out of the ordinary, I'll find out."

"And we'll talk to Mia," Ruby added. "She's been monitoring security. If anyone's been accessing restricted areas, she'll know."

The fire crackled as we fell into a tense silence, each of us lost in our thoughts. The betrayal felt like a shadow creeping through the walls of the estate, cold and insidious.

Later that evening, Ruby and I met Mia in the control room. Screens displayed live feeds of the estate, the glow of the monitors casting an eerie light over her focused face.

"I've already started going through the logs," Mia said as we entered. "No unusual activity on the external cameras, but... there's something odd about the internal system."

I frowned, stepping closer to the screen she was pointing at. "What kind of odd?"

"Someone accessed the network last night, just before the shipment was compromised. They didn't leave a clear trail, but it was someone with high-level clearance."

"Which means it's someone in the house," Ruby said, her voice tight.

Mia nodded. "I've narrowed it down to a handful of possible users, but I need more time to pinpoint exactly who it was."

"Do it," I said. "And don't tell anyone else about this. The last thing we need is for the traitor to know we're onto them."

Mia's jaw tightened. "You've got it. But Ryan... whoever this is, they're smart. They know how to cover their tracks. It's not going to be easy." I placed a hand on her shoulder. "Just do what you can. We'll handle the rest."

The confrontation came sooner than I expected. It was late, the estate quiet save, for the faint hum of the security systems. I was making my way back to the study when I heard raised voices coming from the kitchen. I rounded the corner to find Leo standing face-to-face with one of the staff—a young man named Peter who'd been with us for nearly a year.

"I swear, I didn't do anything!" Peter's voice cracked, his eyes wide with fear. "I don't know how they got the information!"

"Then explain this!" Leo growled, holding up a small flash drive.

"What's going on?" I demanded, stepping into the room.

Leo turned to me, his expression furious. "I found this in Peter's locker. It's got schematics for the shipment routes." My blood ran cold. "Peter, what the hell is this?" Peter shook his head frantically. "It's not mine! I don't know how it got there! You must believe me, Mr. Giovannetti!" Ruby appeared in the doorway, her eyes darting between us. "What's happening?" Leo didn't take his eyes off Peter. "We've got our traitor."

"No!" Peter cried. "I'm being set up! I swear, I'd never betray you!"

Ruby stepped forward, her voice calm but firm. "Peter, if you didn't do this, then who did? Who would want to frame you?"

"I... I don't know," Peter stammered, tears welling in his eyes. "But I swear, I'm loyal to this family. Please, you must believe me!"

I studied him closely, searching for any sign of deceit. His fear seemed genuine, but the evidence was damning. Ruby touched my arm. "Ryan, we need to be sure. If he's telling the truth..." I nodded, my jaw tightening. "Leo, lock down the estate. No one comes or goes until we get to the bottom of this." As Leo led Peter away, Ruby and I exchanged a look. The fracture in our circle was deeper than I'd realized, and the consequences of this betrayal were only just beginning to unfold. The house was quieter than usual, the tension thick enough to choke on. Every creak of the floorboards, every distant murmur felt amplified in the suffocating silence. Ruby and I sat in the study, the fire in the hearth burning low. The room was dim, the flickering light casting long shadows on the walls. Ruby leaned forward, her elbows resting on her knees, her brow furrowed in thought. "Peter seemed terrified," she said, breaking the silence. "If he's guilty, he's the best actor I've ever seen."

I rubbed my hands over my face, exhaustion weighing down on me like a lead blanket. "I don't know what to believe. The flash drive in his locker is damning, but the fear in his eyes wasn't fake. If he's being set up, someone's going to a lot of trouble to make him look guilty." Ruby sat back, her gaze locking with mine. "We need to be careful, Ryan. If there's someone else pulling the strings, we can't let them manipulate us into turning against each other." Her words struck a chord. Whoever was behind this wasn't just after information—they were trying to dismantle us from the inside out. It was a tactic my father had used more times than I cared to remember. Divide and conquer. And it worked.

> "We need to talk to Judie," I said finally. "She's seen these kinds of games before. She might have insight we're missing."

Ruby nodded, standing and pulling me up with her. "Let's go."

We found Judie in the solarium, her favourite retreat when the stress of the day became too much. She was sipping tea, her back straight, her demeanour calm despite the storm raging within the house. When we entered, she looked up, her sharp eyes assessing us instantly. "You look like you've been run over by a truck," she said, her tone dry but laced with concern. I managed a weak smile. "It's been one of those days." Judie set her teacup down and gestured for us to sit. "Let me guess—Peter?" Ruby nodded. "Leo found a flash drive in his locker with the shipment schematics. Peter swears he's being framed." Judie's lips pressed into a thin line, her expression unreadable. "And what do you think?"

> "I think it's too convenient," I admitted. "Peter doesn't strike me as someone who'd risk everything to betray us. But the evidence is there."

Judie leaned back, her eyes narrowing in thought. "If someone is framing him, they've done their homework. A flash drive in his locker? That's amateur hour if you ask me. It's almost too obvious."

> "Exactly," Ruby said. "Whoever planted it wanted us to find it. They're playing a game."

Judie's gaze flicked to me. "And how are you planning to play back, Ryan?" I hesitated. "We've locked down the estate. No one leaves until we figure out who's behind this. Mia's combing through security logs, and Leo's interrogating the staff." Judie shook her head. "That's reactive. You need to be proactive. If they're setting traps, you need to spring them on your terms, not theirs." Ruby frowned. "What are you suggesting?" Judie's eyes gleamed with a dangerous edge. "Use the bait they've given you. Let them think their plan is working. If they believe you've fallen for their frame job, they'll get sloppy." I exchanged a look with Ruby. "Set a trap of our own." Judie nodded. "Exactly. But it has to be airtight. One wrong move, and they'll see through it."

Later that night, Ruby and I sat on the edge of our bed, discussing the plan. The storm outside had quieted, leaving an eerie calm in its wake.

"Do you think this will work?" Ruby asked, her voice soft.

"It has to," I said. "Whoever's behind this is trying to tear us apart from the inside. If we don't stop them now, they'll keep pushing until we're too broken to fight back."

Ruby placed her hand on mine, her touch a steadying force. "We'll get through this, Ryan. Together."

I turned to her, my chest tightening with gratitude and love. "I don't deserve you, you know that?" She smiled, leaning in to rest her forehead against mine. "No, you don't. But you've got me anyway." Her words were a balm to the chaos swirling in my mind. No matter what happened, I knew we could face it together. The next morning, the estate buzzed with an uneasy energy. The staff moved about with hushed urgency, casting wary glances at one another. The walls felt like they were closing in, the atmosphere saturated with suspicion. Ruby and I made our way to the central courtyard, where Leo was waiting. His stance was rigid, his arms crossed, and his eyes sharp. Behind him,

Peter sat on a bench, his head in his hands, looking every bit the picture of defeat.

"How's it going?" I asked, keeping my voice neutral.

Leo glanced back at Peter before answering. "He hasn't said much. Claims he doesn't know how the flash drive ended up in his locker." Peter lifted his head at that, his eyes pleading. "Because I don't know! I swear to you, I didn't do this, Mr. Giovannetti. I've been loyal—always." I studied him carefully. Every word seemed genuine, his desperation palpable. But genuine wasn't the same as truthful.

"Peter," I said, stepping closer. Ruby stayed by my side, her presence grounding me. "I want to believe you. But you understand how this looks, don't you? The flash drive, the schematics—it's a perfect setup."

Peter's face twisted with frustration. "That's exactly what it is! A setup! Someone planted it to make me look guilty. Why would I risk everything? My family, my life here—it doesn't make sense." Ruby spoke then, her voice firm but kind. "If you're telling the truth, then we'll find out who's behind this. But we need your help. Think back—has anything seemed off lately? Anyone acting strange? Any threats?" Peter's brows knitted together as he thought. After a moment, he hesitated. "There was something. Last week, I noticed one of the supply manifests had been altered. It was subtle—just a small change to the inventory list. I thought it was a mistake, but when I went to double-check, the original document was missing." My jaw tightened. "Why didn't you report this?"

"I... I didn't think it was important," Peter admitted, his voice barely above a whisper. "I didn't want to waste anyone's time over what might've been nothing."

Leo let out a sharp breath, clearly irritated. "That 'nothing' might've been the first sign of this entire setup." Peter's face crumpled further, shame etched into his features. "I'm sorry. I should've said something." Ruby touched my arm, her eyes meeting mine. "This could be the lead we need. If someone's tampering with the manifests, we might be able to trace it back to them." I nodded. "Mia's been combing through the security logs. If there's a connection, she'll find it. For now, Peter, you stay where we can see you. You're not going anywhere until we get to the bottom of this." Peter's shoulders sagged, but he nodded. "I understand. I just want to clear my name."

The silence stretched thin, suffocating, as Leo paced near the fireplace, his hands clenched into tight fists. Ruby sat next to me on the couch, her hand gripping mine like a lifeline. Across the room, Mia was staring down at her tablet, her expression unusually grim. She'd been working nonstop since we'd discovered the breach, trying to piece together what had gone wrong.

And then she looked up, her voice cutting through the tension like a knife. "We found him." I felt a flicker of hope—a foolish, desperate thing. "Peter?" Mia nodded, but the pain in her eyes told me what I didn't want to hear. "He's dead, Ryan." The words hit me like a physical blow, stealing the breath from my lungs. Ruby gasped softly beside me, her fingers tightening around mine.

"How?" I managed to ask, though the answer didn't matter. Dead was dead.

Mia hesitated, glancing at Leo before continuing. "It was staged to look like an accident—car crash on the outskirts of town. But..." She swallowed hard. "It wasn't an accident. The autopsy showed blunt force trauma to the back of his head. Whoever did this wanted it to look clean, but they didn't care enough to cover all their tracks."

"Are you saying this was an execution?" Ruby asked, her voice trembling with shock and anger.

Mia nodded, her jaw tight. "Yes. Whoever got to Peter didn't just use him; they eliminated him. Probably to tie up loose ends." I stood abruptly, pulling away from Ruby's touch as the anger roared to life inside me. "He was one of us. He was supposed to be safe here. How the hell did this happen?"

"Because someone inside let it happen," Leo said, his voice low but seething with barely restrained fury. "We have a mole, Ryan. And they're playing us."

The room felt colder now, the walls pressing in as the implications of Leo's words settled over us. Peter hadn't just been a casualty; he'd been a message.

Ruby rose to her feet, stepping in front of me. Her eyes burned with determination. "We can't let this tear us apart, Ryan. That's exactly what they want. We need to stay strong, stay together. If we let this break us, they win." Her words grounded me, pulling me back from the brink of my rage. I cupped her face in my hands, searching her eyes for strength—and finding it.

"We'll figure out who's behind this," I promised her, my voice steady despite the storm raging inside me. "And when we do, they'll regret ever coming after us."

Mia cleared her throat, drawing our attention back to her. "I'll keep digging into Peter's movements before his death. If he was coerced into this, there might be clues we can follow."

"Do it," I said, my tone firm. "And double the security measures. I don't want another body turning up under our watch."

Leo nodded, already pulling out his phone to make calls. "I'll get the team on it. We'll find this mole, Ryan. And when we do..."

"We'll make them pay," I finished, my voice cold and resolute.

Ruby slid her hand back into mine, her grip firm. "Together." Together. It was the only way we'd survive this. But as I stared into the flames licking the hearth, I couldn't shake the image of Peter's face—the fear he must have felt in his final moments. Whoever had done this would learn soon enough: when you came after my family, there was always a price to pay. And I would make damn sure they paid it in full.

Back in the control room, Mia sat at her station, screens glowing with lines of code and surveillance footage. She glanced up as we entered, her expression focused.

"Got something for me?" I asked.

Mia nodded, motioning us closer. "I've been digging into the footage near Peter's locker. Look at this." She tapped a few keys, and a grainy video played on the main screen. A figure in dark clothing moved quickly down the hallway, their face obscured by a hood. They stopped near Peter's locker, fiddling with something, then walked away.

"Do we have a clear shot of their face?" Ruby asked, leaning forward.

Mia shook her head. "They knew where the cameras were. Kept their head down the whole time. But..." She tapped the keyboard again, zooming in on the footage. "Look at their wrist. Right there." On the figure's wrist was a bracelet—a thin, silver chain with a distinctive charm dangling from it.

"I've seen that bracelet before," Ruby said, her tone sharp.

"So have I," I said, the realization hitting me like a punch to the gut.

The bracelet belonged to Elena, one of the newer staff members. She'd been hired only a few months ago, her background check spotless.

"It can't be a coincidence," Ruby said, her voice laced with frustration. "She's been planted here."

"Looks like it," Mia agreed. "Want me to bring her in?"

I shook my head. "Not yet. If she's working for someone, we need to find out who. Let's set the trap." Ruby's eyes met mine, her resolve matching my own. "It's time to turn the tables." Elena's bracelet burned in my mind as we left the control room. It wasn't just a piece of jewellery anymore—it was a link to whoever had orchestrated Peter's betrayal, a clue dangling right in front of us. Ruby walked beside me, her silence heavier than usual. She was thinking, analysing, preparing.

"I don't like this," she finally said, her voice low. "If Elena is working for someone, they might already know we're onto her."

"She won't know we've connected the dots," I assured her, though the words felt thin. "Not yet."

Ruby stopped me in the hallway, her hands gripping my forearms. "Ryan, this is dangerous. If she's planted here, she's already proven she's good at hiding. We can't underestimate her—or whoever she's working for." I placed my hands over hers, grounding myself in her presence. "We'll handle it together. I won't let her or anyone else blindside us." Ruby nodded, but her worry didn't fade. I didn't blame her. We'd both seen how fast trust could be weaponized. When we reached the main floor, Leo was waiting in the lounge, his arms crossed. "Mia filled me in," he said without preamble. "We've got a mole, and you want to play it subtle?"

"For now," I said, keeping my voice calm. "If we corner her too soon, we lose any chance of finding out who she's working for."

Leo's jaw tightened, but he nodded. "What's the plan?" I glanced at Ruby. She gave me a small nod, letting me take the lead. "We'll act like nothing's wrong. Keep her in her routine but watch her closely. Mia will monitor her movements, and we'll start feeding her false information—something that'll flush out her handler."

Leo's brows rose. "Risky. You're banking on her handler biting."

"They will," Ruby interjected. "They need her to succeed, and they'll want to stay ahead of us. But it only works if we stay sharp."

Leo sighed, running a hand through his hair. "Fine. I'll make sure the staff keeps their distance. No need for anyone else to complicate things." As Leo left, Ruby and I moved toward the courtyard. It was empty now, the string lights swaying gently in the evening breeze. I could feel the tension radiating off Ruby as we sat on one of the benches, the quiet between us stretching.

"Do you think Peter knew?" she asked suddenly, her voice barely above a whisper.

I shook my head. "No. He didn't strike me as someone who'd willingly sell us out. He was scared—probably got manipulated or threatened." Ruby frowned, her gaze fixed on the reflection pond in the distance. "And now he's gone. Whoever's behind this isn't afraid to tie up loose ends."

"That's why we have to move fast," I said, my tone firm. "If Elena's just a piece of the puzzle, we need to see the whole picture before they make their next move."

Ruby leaned into me, her head resting on my shoulder. "Promise me something."

"Anything."

"No matter how this plays out, we don't let them tear us apart. Not like this."

I turned to look at her, my hand gently cupping her cheek. "Nothing will. Not now, not ever." She smiled softly, but her eyes held the weight of everything we were facing. "Then let's finish this." The next morning, Mia briefed us on Elena's movements. She'd gone about her duties as usual, seemingly unaware that the walls were closing in around her. But I knew better. People like her, people who played this game, were always watching, always waiting for the slightest shift in the air. Ruby and I entered the dining hall where Elena was setting the table for breakfast. She looked up, her expression polite, but her eyes flicked over us, calculating.

"Good morning, Mr. and Mrs. Giovannetti," she said with a practiced smile.

I forced a smile in return. "Good morning, Elena. Everything ready for the staff meeting later?" She hesitated, just a fraction of a second, but it was enough. "Of course, sir. I'll make sure everything's set." Ruby stepped forward, her tone light. "You've been such a help lately, Elena. It's good to know we can rely on you." Elena's smile faltered, just slightly. "Thank you, Mrs. Giovannetti. I take pride in my work." As we left the room, I caught Ruby's knowing glance. "She's nervous," she murmured. "Did you see the way her hand twitched when you mentioned the meeting?"

"She's feeling the pressure," I agreed. "Now we wait and see how she reacts."

That night, Mia sent us an alert. Elena had left her quarters and was heading toward the staff exit, her pace quick. Ruby and I joined Leo near the security monitors.

"She's meeting someone," Mia said, her voice clipped. "She's carrying a small bag—looks like she's delivering something."

"Where's she going?" I asked.

Mia pulled up the exterior cameras, showing Elena slipping through the estate's gates. "She's heading toward the main road."

"Time to follow," Ruby said, already moving toward the door.

I grabbed her arm gently. "We stick to the plan. We need to see who she's meeting." Ruby hesitated, then nodded. We watched as Elena disappeared into the night, the trap we'd set tightening around her. Whoever she was working for, whatever they wanted—it was time to bring it all to light.

Tides of Vengeance

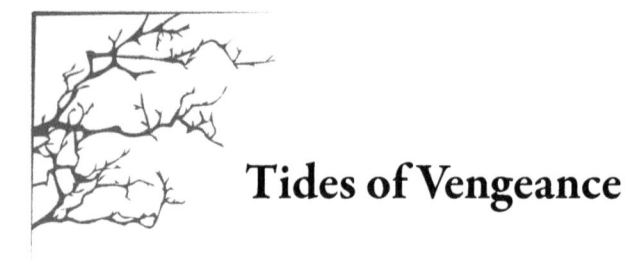

The silence between Ruby and me as we stood in the hallway of the estate was almost suffocating. We'd just learned everything we needed to know about Elena's movements, and yet it felt like we were standing at the edge of something far deeper, far more dangerous than we'd anticipated. Peter's death still hung over us like a storm cloud, casting a shadow on every decision we made. Whoever had orchestrated his betrayal wasn't just sending a message—they were playing a long game, one where the stakes were higher than we could have imagined. The cost of this war, of vengeance, would be steep. It already had been.

> "Ryan, what's the next move?" Ruby's voice broke the silence, but her words felt heavy, like she knew that whatever came next, it wouldn't be easy. "Elena's not the only one we need to watch. Whoever she's working for... they've been ahead of us this whole time."

I looked at her, seeing the worry in her eyes. The fear that something would pull us apart, something we couldn't control. But I couldn't let that happen. Not now, not ever.

> "First, we make sure Elena doesn't realize we're on to her," I said, my voice steady but tired. "We keep her close. Let her think we're still buying the story she's selling. But we move fast. The longer we wait, the more dangerous this becomes."

Ruby nodded, though there was still a shadow in her gaze. She'd been through too much with me to ever let me take the weight of it all without a fight. But I saw her resolve, too. She understood what had to be done. As we entered the living room, Leo stood by the window, his posture tense. The look on his face told me he wasn't in the mood for small talk.

"We've got a situation," Leo said, his voice sharp, eyes flicking between Ruby and me. "Mia's tracking Elena, and she's not sticking to her usual patterns. She's getting more erratic—almost like she knows we're watching her."

I exhaled slowly, the tension in my chest tightening. "She's good at covering her tracks. Whoever she's working for, they're still one step ahead of us."

"We need a new approach," Ruby said, her voice calm but firm. "We can't keep playing this game of cat and mouse. We need to confront her—make her reveal who's pulling the strings. But we need to make sure we have the leverage."

Leo frowned, his arms crossed tightly. "You're thinking of getting more aggressive?"

"I'm thinking we need to force her hand," I said, my voice low. "We don't have the luxury of time. Peter's dead. And whoever killed him won't hesitate to take us out too. We must make a move before they make another one."

Ruby stepped closer, her presence grounding me. "We need to be smart about this. If we're too direct, we risk tipping our hand. But if we wait too long..."

"The cost will be too high," I finished for her.

The weight of our plan settled in, but we both knew it was the only option. Elena was the key to uncovering who was behind Peter's death—and everything else that had been set into motion. But we couldn't just storm in and demand answers. This wasn't a battle of brute force—it was a game of strategy, of knowing when to push and when to retreat.

"We need to keep our options open," I said, turning back to Leo. "If we put too much pressure on Elena, she'll fold. We need to catch her off guard. Let her make the next move."

Leo nodded, but I could see the frustration in his eyes. "It's risky. But we don't have much choice."

"We'll start with small moves," I said, more to myself than to anyone else. "Find out who's in contact with her. Whoever's running this game—whoever killed Peter—they're close. Too close."

Ruby squeezed my arm. "And when we find them, we'll make sure they pay for what they've done." I looked down at her, seeing the fire in her eyes. I knew we were both thinking the same thing. The lines between justice and vengeance had blurred a long time ago. And now, they were leading us down a dangerous path where the stakes were too high to ignore. The sound of the door opening pulled my attention away from Ruby, and Mia stepped into the room, her expression unreadable.

"I've got something," Mia said, holding out a folder. "We've been tracking Elena's movements more closely, and I think I've found something important."

I took the folder, flipping it open. Inside, there was a list of names, phone numbers, and timestamps—all linked to Elena's recent movements. It wasn't much, but it was a start.

"There's one name here," Mia continued, pointing to a number. "It's tied to a series of calls she's made in the last few days. It's someone who's connected to the Romano family."

My heart skipped. Dante Romano. The name was enough to make everything fall into place.

"Elena's been working for him the whole time," I said, my mind racing. "We've been dealing with more than just a mole. This is bigger than I thought."

Ruby's expression hardened. "Romano's been running things in the shadows for years. If he's behind this, we're not just dealing with a betrayal. We're dealing with an all-out war." I nodded, the realization hitting me like a punch to the gut. This was no longer just about uncovering a traitor. This was about survival.

"We move on Romano," I said, my voice firm. "We bring him down, and we end this."

The air felt heavier than usual as we regrouped in the estate's control room. The revelation of Dante Romano's involvement changed everything. Romano was a ghost—a figure who thrived in the shadows, orchestrating chaos from the sidelines. And now, he was in our crosshairs. Ruby stood at the centre of the room, her arms crossed tightly over her chest, her mind visibly working through the next steps. Leo leaned against the far wall, his jaw clenched, while Mia worked furiously at the computer, pulling up every scrap of data she could find.

"We need a direct approach," Leo said, breaking the tense silence. "Romano doesn't play fair, and he won't hesitate to strike first. If we wait, we'll lose whatever advantage we have."

"We can't just rush in blind," Ruby countered. Her tone was sharp but calm, cutting through the tension like a blade. "Romano's not someone you corner without a plan. We need to find his weak spot—something we can use to bring him down."

Mia turned from her screen, her face illuminated by the blue light. "He's been careful to keep his operations hidden, but there's one thing that stands out. Romano has a meeting scheduled in two days at an old estate just outside the city. It's heavily secured, but if he's there in person, it means it's important." My gaze locked on the map Mia displayed on the monitor. The location was secluded, surrounded by dense forest—a fortress designed to keep intruders out and secrets in.

"It's a risk," I said, stepping forward. "But if Romano's going to be there, it's our best shot at getting answers. And if Elena's part of this, she'll lead us right to him."

Ruby turned to me, her brow furrowed. "If we go in, we need to be ready for anything. This isn't just about Romano. If he's working with others, we're walking into the lion's den."

"That's why we do it on our terms," I said. "We don't just show up—we make sure he doesn't see us coming. Mia, can you intercept their security systems? Disrupt their communications?"

Mia smirked, her fingers flying over the keyboard. "Consider it done. I'll have their entire network in the palm of my hand. But it won't hold for long. You'll need to move fast."

Leo straightened, his expression dark. "We'll go in small. Just us. No backup, no additional staff. We can't risk anyone else getting caught in the crossfire." Ruby nodded, her resolve unwavering. "And if Elena's there, we take her alive. We need her to talk." The room fell silent as the weight of the plan settled over us. We were walking a razor's edge, and every decision carried the risk of everything falling apart.

"Alright," I said finally. "We move tomorrow night. We'll monitor Elena until then, make sure she doesn't suspect anything. And when the time comes, we end this."

I leaned against the hood of the black SUV as Leo pulled up beside me, the cool night air whispering through the secluded meeting spot just outside the city. The plan was in motion, but Ruby's absence weighed heavily on me. She'd insisted on staying behind, knowing this mission carried too much risk. It was one of the unspoken agreements we had: I'd keep her away from the crossfire, and she'd handle the delicate balance of negotiations when the time came. Mia's voice crackled through the comms. "Elena's tracker shows she's two miles from the drop location. You've got maybe ten minutes to get in position." Leo stepped out of the vehicle, slipping on his gloves. "She doesn't know we're here?"

"She's being careful," Mia replied. "But no signs she suspects anything. The tracker's holding steady."

I nodded and glanced at Leo. "We stick to the plan. No unnecessary risks. We need Elina alive." He smirked faintly. "Your restraint is admirable. Let's hope it holds."

We moved into position, the shadows of the abandoned warehouse covering us. Elena's handler was the key to unravelling this entire betrayal, and tonight, we'd force their hand.

Back at the estate, Ruby paced in the study, her phone clutched in her hand. She hated being sidelined, but we both knew the dangers of her being out here tonight. Negotiation was her battlefield; this was mine. Mia's voice over the private line kept her updated. "They're in position. Elena is approaching the warehouse." Ruby's heart clenched. "And Ryan?"

"Calm, focused, ready," Mia assured her. "You trained him for this, remember?"

Ruby's lips pressed into a thin line. "That doesn't make it easier."

Elena arrived at the abandoned warehouse, her steps precise and cautious. The dim light from a single hanging bulb illuminated the shadows, but it wasn't enough to erase the tension etched on her face. She glanced around, her hand brushing the bracelet on her wrist—a nervous tic we'd come to recognize through hours of surveillance. I watched her from the shadows with Leo, the weight of the moment pressing down like a vice. This was it. Mia's voice crackled softly through the comms. "She's not alone. The second party is ten meters out, approaching the south entrance."

"Stay sharp," I murmured to Leo, my grip tightening on the pistol holstered at my side.

The south entrance creaked open, and in stepped Dante Romano. His name alone was enough to make my blood boil. A former enforcer for the Giovannetti empire, Dante had a reputation for brutality and cunning. He'd disappeared after my father's death, leaving behind a trail of whispers that he was building something of his own. Now, seeing him here confirmed those rumours—and tied him to Elena's betrayal.

"Well, well," Dante said, his voice smooth as he approached Elena. "Right on time. I was beginning to think you'd lost your nerve."

Elena straightened, forcing a calm she didn't feel. "I've delivered everything you asked for. The Giovannetti's don't suspect a thing." Dante smirked, his gaze sliding over her like a predator sizing up prey.

"Good. Because if they did, you wouldn't be standing here."

Elena swallowed hard, but before she could respond, Dante's demeanour shifted. "And the security breach? Did it work as planned?"

"Yes," she said quickly. "Peter did what you wanted, but... they found him. They know he's dead."

Dante's expression darkened. "Peter was a necessary sacrifice. He knew the risks, and he failed to cover his tracks. His weakness isn't my problem."

"Then what is?" I said, stepping out of the shadows, my voice sharp and cutting.

Dante turned, his eyes narrowing as he spotted me. Elena's face drained of colour, her hands trembling at her sides.

"Well, if it isn't Ryan Giovannetti," Dante said, his smirk returning. "Still playing the noble leader, I see."

I ignored the jab, my focus on him. "You've been busy, Dante. Sabotaging my estate, killing Peter, manipulating Elena. What's your endgame?" He chuckled, a low, mocking sound. "Endgame? This isn't about games, Ryan. This is about reclaiming what was lost. Your father's empire—it was never yours to inherit."

"Funny," I said, stepping closer. "Because I'm pretty sure I burned that empire to the ground."

Dante's smile faded, replaced by cold fury. "You think you can erase history? The Giovannetti name means something, and I intend to remind the world of that—whether you like it or not."

Leo moved in behind me, his gun trained on Dante. "Drop whatever you're holding, or I'll put you down right now."

Dante raised his hands in mock surrender, but his confidence didn't waver. "You can kill me, Leo. But you won't stop what's coming. The Famiglia Notturno isn't a relic—it's a legacy. And you're either part of it, or you're in its way." Before I could respond, Mia's voice cut through the comms. "Ryan, we've got movement outside—two vehicles inbound, heavily armed." Dante grinned, sensing the shift. "Looks like we've got company. I'd love to stay and chat, but I've got bigger plans tonight." As the sound of tires screeching echoed through the warehouse, Dante threw a smoke canister, the room filling with thick, choking fog. Gunfire erupted, and I grabbed Leo, pulling him into cover.

"Elena!" I shouted, but when the smoke cleared, she was gone, along with Dante.

Leo cursed under his breath. "They were ready for this." I nodded, my jaw clenched. "But so are we."

We retreated, regrouping at the estate where Ruby was waiting in the study. Her eyes locked onto mine the moment I entered, her concern palpable.

"Are you okay?" she asked, her voice steady despite the storm behind her gaze.

"They got away," I admitted, frustration leaking into my tone. "But now we know who we're dealing with."

"Dante," she said, the name like venom on her lips. "He's trying to rebuild your father's empire."

"Not if I can help it," I said, sitting down beside her. "He's underestimated us before. He won't do it again."

Ruby reached for my hand, her grip firm. "We'll find him. And when we do, he'll learn exactly what happens when he threatens what we've built." I nodded, her strength grounding me. Together, we would unravel Dante's plans—and this time, there would be no escape for him. The quiet of the estate was deceptive. Every corner hummed with tension as our team prepared for the next step. Dante's reappearance wasn't just a threat; it was a declaration of war. The man wasn't just ambitious—he was reckless, and reckless enemies were always the most dangerous. Ruby sat beside me in the study, her tablet open as she scrolled through Mia's latest updates on Dante's network. Her focus was razor-sharp, and even though this wasn't her battlefield, her presence was a constant reminder of why I fought so hard. For her. For us.

"His movements have been erratic," Ruby said, her brow furrowing. "He's not staying in one place for long."

"He knows we'll be looking for him," I replied. "He won't make it easy."

Leo entered the room, a folder in hand. He tossed it onto the table with a grim expression. "Dante's been reaching out to old allies. Some of them aren't happy about it, but others... well, they're listening." I flipped open the folder, scanning the profiles of familiar faces from my past. Names I'd hoped never to see again. "We need to cut off his support before it solidifies. If he gathers enough allies, it'll be a full-blown resurgence." Ruby looked up, her gaze piercing. "And Elena? What's her next move?"

"She's the key," Leo said. "She's feeding him information, and she's too valuable for him to cut loose. If we find her, we'll find him."

Mia's voice came through the intercom. "I might have something. Surveillance picked up Elena leaving the city limits, heading west. She made a stop at a remote airfield about an hour ago."

"West?" Leo asked, frowning. "That's out of his usual range. What's out there?"

"A lot of nothing," Mia said. "But there's a private hangar registered under a shell company that traces back to Dante. It's a likely rendezvous point."

I pushed to my feet, adrenaline surging. "Then that's where we'll find her." Ruby's eyes narrowed, her grip tightening on the tablet. "What's the plan?" I hesitated, knowing what she was asking. "Ruby—"

"I'm not going on this one," she interrupted, her tone firm.
"I know. But I want to know the plan."

Relief and gratitude warred within me. Ruby had always understood the risks, but she also knew when to step back. "Leo and I will take a small team. We'll intercept her at the hangar, cut off her escape, and bring her in. Mia will coordinate from here."

"And what happens if Dante's there?" she asked, her voice steady but laced with concern.

"Then we finish this," I said, my tone resolute.

Ruby studied me for a moment, then nodded. "Just come back. All of you." I leaned down, pressing a kiss to her forehead. "Always."

The drive to the airfield was quiet, save for the hum of the engine and the occasional crackle of the comms. Leo sat beside me, his rifle resting across his lap.

"Think he'll show?" Leo asked, his tone grim.

"He's cocky," I replied. "If he thinks he's untouchable, he'll make an appearance."

Leo snorted. "Then let's make sure he regrets it." When we arrived, the hangar was eerily still, its towering doors closed. The only light came from a single bulb near the entrance, casting long shadows across the gravel lot. Mia's voice came through the comms.

"Elena's inside. Heat signatures confirm at least four others with her, but no sign of Dante. If he's there, he's staying out of sight."

"Copy that," I said. "We go in quiet. No one leaves until we get answers."

Leo and the team spread out, circling the hangar as I approached the side entrance. The door creaked open with a light push, revealing a cavernous interior filled with crates and vehicles. Elena stood near the centre, speaking with a man I didn't recognize. Two others lingered nearby, armed but distracted.

"Elena," I called, stepping into the light.

She froze, her head snapping toward me. Panic flared in her eyes, but she quickly masked it, her hands clenching at her sides. "Mr. Giovannetti. I wasn't expecting you."

"I bet," I said, my voice cold. "We need to talk."

The man beside her reached for his weapon, but Leo's voice rang out. "Don't even think about it." From the shadows, my team emerged, weapons trained on the group. The armed men dropped their guns, their expressions hard. Elena backed up a step, her composure cracking.

"You've been busy," I said, closing the distance between us. "Betrayal. Espionage. And now what? Running to Dante like a loyal lapdog?"

Her mask shattered, fear and defiance warring in her gaze. "You don't understand—"

"Then explain it to me," I snapped. "Because from where I'm standing, you've made your choices."

Before she could respond, the sound of engines roared to life outside. Mia's voice crackled through the comms. "Ryan, we've got incoming—two SUVs, heavily armed."

"Dante," Leo muttered, his grip tightening on his rifle.

I turned back to Elena, my voice low and sharp. "This is your last chance. Who's pulling the strings?"

Her lips parted, but before she could speak, a shot rang out, shattering the stillness. Elena crumpled to the ground, a crimson stain spreading across her chest.

"Sniper!" Leo shouted, dragging me into cover as chaos erupted.

Dante's voice echoed through the hangar, cold and mocking. "You should've stayed out of this, Ryan." I clenched my teeth, adrenaline surging. This wasn't over. Not by a long shot.

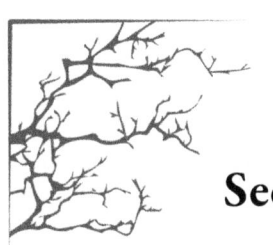

Secrets in the Dark

The echo of Dante's voice lingered in the hangar, a cruel taunt that sent my pulse racing. Elena's lifeless body lay crumpled on the ground, her betrayal silenced in an instant. But her death raised more questions than it answered.

"Stay down!" Leo barked, his voice cutting through the chaos as he scanned for the sniper.

Mia's voice came through the comms, tense but steady. "Snipers positioned southwest of the hangar. Thermal shows they're moving—looks like they're packing up."

"Dante's men?" I asked, gripping my sidearm tightly.

"Most likely. The SUVs are repositioning too, trying to block off the exit," Mia confirmed.

Leo swore under his breath. "They're boxing us in."

"Not for long," I said, motioning to the rest of the team. "Mia, relay coordinates for the sniper to Leo's team. Everyone else, we move to secure the SUVs. Dante doesn't leave this airfield."

As we moved through the hangar, the sharp tang of gunpowder filled the air. Leo's men engaged the sniper's position, suppressing fire echoing in the distance. I led the way toward the exit, Ruby's earlier warnings replaying in my mind.

"This is dangerous. You can't underestimate them."

She'd been right, as always. And though she wasn't here, her voice steadied me, reminding me why we couldn't afford to lose. The SUVs were waiting near the edge of the lot, their headlights cutting through the night. Armed men stood at the ready, their weapons trained on the hangar. But they weren't prepared for the full force of our retaliation. I signalled the team, and we split into two groups, flanking the vehicles. The crack of gunfire erupted as we closed in, taking out their tires and neutralizing their drivers. One of the men tried to retreat, but I caught him with a clean shot to the leg, sending him sprawling to the ground.

"Where's Dante?" I demanded, pinning him with my foot as he writhed in pain.

He gritted his teeth, defiance gleaming in his eyes. "You'll never catch him. He's always one step ahead." I pressed harder. "Where?" Before he could answer, another SUV roared to life, speeding away from the lot. My heart clenched as I recognized the figure in the passenger seat—Dante.

"Leo!" I called, pointing toward the fleeing vehicle.

"On it!" he shouted, breaking off with two men to give chase.

I turned back to the injured man, crouching beside him. "Talk, or I make sure you regret it." He sneered, blood staining his teeth. "You think killing me will stop him? You don't know what you're up against."

"I'm done playing games," I said, my patience snapping.

"Who's he working with? Francesca? Vitale? Mancini?"

The man laughed, a guttural sound that made my stomach turn. "You're chasing ghosts. Francesca and Vitale don't answer to anyone—not even Dante." I grabbed his collar, my voice dropping to a deadly whisper. "Then who's pulling the strings?" His gaze flicked toward the hangar, where Elena's body still lay. "You'll find out soon enough. But it won't matter. You're already too late." I released him, disgust churning in my gut. His cryptic warning only deepened the pit forming in my stomach.

Back at the Estate

The debrief was tense, the team on edge after the botched operation. Dante had slipped through our fingers, and the sniper's escape left too many loose ends. But the biggest blow was Elena—her betrayal and death weighed heavily on all of us. Mia projected a map of the region onto the wall, marking the SUV's last known trajectory. "We tracked Dante's vehicle to the industrial district, but the signal went dark before we could pinpoint his location."

"He's regrouping," Leo said, his arms crossed. "Probably rallying what's left of his forces."

"Or laying a trap," I said. "Dante doesn't run unless he's got a plan."

Ruby entered the room, her expression unreadable as she approached me. She placed a hand on my arm, her touch grounding me.

"What's next?" she asked softly.

I met her gaze, the weight of our situation reflected in her eyes. "We dig deeper. Mancini's still out there, and now we know Francesca and Vitale are involved. We find them, and we cut them off at the source." Ruby nodded, but her worry didn't fade. "And what about Dante? He won't stop coming for us."

"I know," I said. "But this time, we'll be ready."

As the room emptied, Ruby lingered beside me, her fingers tracing absent patterns along my arm. "Ryan," she said after a long silence, "there's something you're not telling me." I tensed, the words catching in my throat. She was right—there was a part of this I hadn't shared. But it wasn't just about protecting her. It was about protecting us.

"I'll tell you everything," I said finally. "But not tonight."

Her eyes searched mine, and after a moment, she nodded. "Just promise me one thing."

"Anything."

"Whatever secrets you're carrying, don't let them destroy us."

I pulled her close, the weight of her words pressing against my chest. "I won't let that happen. Not now, not ever." But as I held her, the shadows of my past crept closer, threatening to tear apart everything we'd fought to build. The estate felt heavy that night, shadows pooling in every corner as if echoing the secrets weighing on my mind. Ruby had gone to bed, leaving me alone in the study with a glass of whiskey and my thoughts. Elena's death, Dante's escape, and the cryptic warning from his man played on a loop in my head.

"You're chasing ghosts..."

The names of Francesca D'Alessandro, Alessandro Vitale, and Giovanni Mancini had resurfaced like Specters from another life, each one tied to a chapter I'd hoped was closed. But Dante's moves weren't random; he was spinning a web that connected my past to the war we were now facing. A knock at the door broke the silence.

"Come in," I called, setting the glass down.

Mia stepped inside, her expression grim. "We've got movement on Mancini." I straightened. "What kind of movement?"

> "He surfaced at one of his old haunts—a private club in the city. Our sources say he's been meeting with intermediaries from Francesca's network." She paused, her jaw tightening. "There's more. We intercepted chatter that Mancini's meeting with Dante tonight. Location's still unclear, but it's happening soon."

I exhaled sharply, the tension in my chest coiling tighter. "Then we can't wait. If they're consolidating power, this is our chance to cut them off." Mia hesitated, her fingers brushing the edge of the door. "Ryan...

there's something else. I ran a trace on that bracelet Elena was wearing. It's not just a tracker—it's encrypted with biometric data. Whoever gave it to her wanted to monitor her every move. It's... sophisticated."

"Too sophisticated for Dante," I muttered, the pieces clicking into place. "It's Francesca's handiwork. She always had a taste for tech."

Mia nodded. "If we decrypt it, we might find out more—locations, communications, maybe even how she connects to Dante and Mancini." I stood, the urgency pulling me forward. "Get started on the decryption. I'll take Leo and the team to intercept Mancini." Mia's brow furrowed.

"What about Ruby? You're not telling her?"
"She stays out of this one," I said firmly. "It's too dangerous."

In the City

The club was a fortress of opulence, hidden behind tinted glass and guarded by men who looked like they'd snap a neck without blinking. Leo and I waited in an alley across the street, the rest of the team positioned strategically around the perimeter.

"Mancini's inside," Leo said, peering through a pair of binoculars. "Looks like he's meeting someone in one of the VIP rooms. Can't confirm Dante yet."

I nodded, adjusting the earpiece. "We move in quietly. No casualties unless necessary. I want Mancini alive." Leo smirked. "You always did ask for miracles." The plan was simple: infiltrate the club, extract Mancini, and gather intel on Francesca and Dante's operations. But simple rarely meant easy. As we slipped through the back entrance, the thrum of bass vibrated through the walls. The main floor was packed, bodies moving to the rhythm of music while oblivious to the predators weaving among them. Leo gestured toward the stairs leading to the VIP section. "Two guards posted. How do you want to handle it?" I scanned the room, my gaze landing on a server carrying a tray of drinks. "Distract them," I said, motioning for him to follow my lead. Leo feigned a stumble, sending the server's tray crashing to the ground. The guards' attention snapped toward the commotion, giving me the opening I needed to slip past.

The VIP section was quieter, the hum of conversation laced with tension. I spotted Mancini at the far end, seated at a table with two men I didn't recognize. His demeanour was relaxed, but his eyes constantly scanned the room—a predator aware of his precarious position. I stepped into the light, drawing his attention.

"Giovannetti," he said, leaning back in his chair with a smirk. "Didn't expect to see you here."

"I'm full of surprises," I replied, my tone cold.

The men beside him shifted, their hands inching toward their weapons. Mancini raised a hand, stopping them.

"Relax, boys. Ryan and I go way back, don't we?" He gestured to the empty chair across from him. "Have a seat. Let's catch up."

I didn't move. "You've been busy, Mancini. Francesca, Vitale, Dante—planning a little reunion?" He laughed, the sound grating. "Ah, you always did love conspiracy theories. What can I say? I have friends in high places."

"Friends who orchestrate betrayals and execute pawns?" I snapped. "You think I don't know about Peter? Or Elena?"

Mancini's smirk faltered for a fraction of a second before returning.

"Peter made his choices. As for Elena... well, she was always expendable."

Rage flared in my chest, but I kept my composure. "Who's giving the orders, Mancini? Francesca? Or is Dante finally calling the shots?" He leaned forward, his eyes gleaming with malice. "You're barking up the wrong tree, Giovannetti. The game's bigger than you think. Bigger than any of us." Before I could press further, a deafening explosion rocked the building, sending shockwaves through the room. The lights flickered, and chaos erupted as patrons screamed and scattered. Mancini bolted for the exit, but I was faster, tackling him to the ground.

"You're not going anywhere," I growled, pinning him down.

He sneered up at me. "You're too late. The pieces are already in motion."

The sound of approaching footsteps drew my attention. Leo appeared, his rifle at the ready. "Ryan, we've got to move. Whoever did this isn't sticking around." I glanced down at Mancini, the weight of his words sinking in.

"Let's go," I said, dragging him to his feet. "This isn't over."

As we exited the club, the burning wreckage of an SUV illuminated the night sky. The message was clear: Francesca and Dante weren't just one step ahead—they were playing a different game entirely. The SUV's smouldering wreckage reflected in Leo's eyes as he scanned the perimeter, his rifle at the ready. Mancini struggled against my grip, his usual smugness replaced with a flash of panic.

"Let me go," he snarled, his voice raw. "You don't understand what you're dealing with!"

"Oh, I understand perfectly," I snapped, shoving him forward. "You're going to start talking, or you'll wish I'd left you in there."

Leo motioned toward the alley where the extraction vehicle waited. "We've got about five minutes before the cops show up. Let's move." Mancini didn't resist as we hauled him into the back of the armoured SUV, his bravado evaporating under the weight of the moment. The vehicle peeled away from the scene, its reinforced frame shielding us from the chaos we'd left behind.

SAFEHOUSE

The safehouse was a nondescript building on the outskirts of the city, its location scrubbed from any database. Inside, the air was thick with tension as we secured Mancini to a chair in the interrogation room. He glared at me, defiance flickering in his dark eyes. "You're making a mistake, Ryan." I crouched in front of him, my voice low and dangerous. "You're going to tell me everything. Starting with Francesca and Dante. What's their endgame?" Mancini laughed, though it sounded hollow. "You think this is about me? About them? You're blind, Giovannetti. This goes so far beyond the names you know."

"Then educate me," I said, gripping the arms of the chair.

He hesitated, his bravado cracking. "Francesca... she's not just rebuilding the old network. She's creating something new. Bigger. Smarter. And Dante? He's the enforcer. The hammer to her scalpel."

"What's the goal?" Leo demanded from behind me.

Mancini's gaze darted to him, then back to me. "Power. Influence. Control of every piece on the board. They're not just after you—they're after the entire foundation of the families." My mind raced, the weight of his words pressing down. If Francesca and Dante were consolidating power, the implications were staggering.

"And what's your role in this?" I pressed.

He smirked, some of his old arrogance returning. "Let's just say I provide... logistical support. But I'm small potatoes compared to what Francesca's planning." Before I could push further, Mia's voice crackled through the comms.

> "Ryan, we've got a problem. Francesca just went dark—her last known location was a private airstrip near the coast. She's on the move."

I stood, my pulse quickening. "Can you track her?"

"Working on it," Mia replied. "But there's more.

That bracelet we pulled from Elena. I cracked part of the encryption. Francesca wasn't just monitoring her—she was using her as a courier. There's a dead drop tied to her movements." Leo cursed under his breath. "Whatever she was carrying, it's already been delivered." Mancini chuckled, drawing my attention back to him. "You're too late, Giovannetti. Francesca's already three steps ahead of you." I grabbed his collar, yanking him forward. "Where's the drop?" His smirk faltered, fear creeping into his expression. "You think she tells me everything? I don't know—" A sharp knock at the door interrupted him. Mia entered, her face grim. "We've got movement near the estate. A vehicle pulled up to the outer perimeter—two occupants. They're not ours." My gut twisted. Ruby.

"Who?" I demanded.

Mia hesitated. "One's confirmed as Alessandro Vitale." My breath caught. Vitale. Francesca's old lieutenant, thought to be dead after an ambush years ago. If he was at the estate, this was personal.

> "Lock down the estate," I ordered, already moving toward the door. "I'm heading back."

> "Ryan," Mia called, her voice firm. "If Vitale's there, it's a trap. He wouldn't come alone."

I stopped, my hand on the doorknob. "Then I'll Spring it."

The Estate

By the time I arrived, the tension was palpable. The estate was a fortress, every inch of it monitored and secured. But even fortresses could be breached. Ruby met me in the foyer, her eyes sharp and unwavering.

"Vitale's here," she said without preamble.

"Where?"

"In the courtyard. He's alone," she added, her tone sceptical.

I frowned. "And the second occupant?"

"Never left the vehicle," she replied.

I turned to Mia, who had taken over the surveillance station in the corner. "What's Vitale playing at?" She shook her head. "He's just sitting there. No visible weapons, no communication devices."

"Stalling," Leo muttered. "He wants us off-balance."

I nodded, the pieces clicking into place. Vitale's appearance wasn't just a message—it was bait.

"Ruby," I said, turning to her. "Stay here."

Her expression hardened. "Ryan—"

"This isn't a negotiation," I cut in, my tone leaving no room for argument. "If this goes sideways, I need you safe."

She hesitated, then gave a reluctant nod. "Be careful."

I stepped into the courtyard, the cool night air biting against my skin. Vitale stood near the fountain, his hands clasped behind his back, a picture of calm confidence.

"Ryan Giovannetti," he said, his voice smooth and mocking. "You're looking well."

"Can't say the same for you," I replied, keeping my distance.
"Cut the theatrics, Vitale. Why are you here?"

He smiled, the expression chilling. "Francesca wanted to send a message. Consider this... a preview." Before I could react, the estate's power cut out, plunging us into darkness. The sudden darkness enveloped the courtyard, silencing everything but the soft rustle of leaves in the cold night breeze. My hand instinctively went to my sidearm, the weight of it grounding me as my vision adjusted.

"Vitale," I called, my voice cutting through the shadows. "What's your play?"

A low chuckle echoed from the fountain's direction. "Oh, Ryan, this isn't a game. It's a reckoning." The comms crackled in my ear, Mia's voice urgent. "Power's been cut at the source. Backup systems are coming online, but there's interference on the network. I can't access the external cameras."

"Can you pinpoint their location?" I asked, moving toward the nearest pillar for cover.

"Negative. Whoever's doing this knows their way around high-end systems. You're blind out there," Mia replied.

I clenched my jaw, scanning the courtyard for movement. "Keep working on it."

A faint shuffle to my left drew my attention. I shifted my aim, my finger brushing the trigger.

"You're outnumbered," Vitale's voice taunted, his tone moving closer. "Francesca doesn't leave loose ends, Ryan. You know that better than anyone."

From the corner of my eye, I caught a glint of metal—a blade slicing through the dark toward me. I ducked, the knife narrowly missing my face, and fired instinctively. The sharp cry that followed confirmed my shot had hit its mark. The estate's backup generators hummed to life, flooding the courtyard with dim, flickering light. Shadows stretched and shifted as I quickly took stock of my surroundings. Vitale stood near the fountain, a smug grin on his face despite the chaos. Behind him, three figures emerged from the darkness, armed and poised to strike.

"You should've stayed out of Francesca's way," Vitale said, gesturing to his men. "But now, you've forced her hand."

"I'm not the one forcing anything," I countered, levelling my weapon at him. "This ends here."

Vitale's grin widened, but before he could respond, a gunshot echoed from the estate entrance. One of his men fell, clutching his shoulder as Leo appeared, his rifle steady and lethal.

"Sorry we're late," Leo said, stepping into the courtyard with Judie and another operative flanking him.

Vitale's expression darkened. "You think reinforcements will save you? Francesca planned for every contingency."

"Good for her," Leo said, firing off another shot.

The courtyard erupted into chaos as Vitale's men returned fire. I moved swiftly, taking cover behind a low stone wall as bullets ricocheted off the marble. Leo's team pushed forward, their precision breaking the attackers' formation. Vitale, however, didn't flinch. He moved with deliberate calm, retreating toward the gate as his men fell around him.

"You won't win this, Ryan!" he shouted over the gunfire.

I rose from cover, my sights trained on him. "Watch me." A sudden movement from the gate drew my attention. The second occupant from the vehicle—a tall, masked figure—emerged, wielding a high-calibre weapon. They fired, forcing everyone to scatter as the courtyard's stone and metal exploded into shards.

"Mia, we need backup now!" I barked into the comms, ducking behind a pillar as debris rained down.

"Already in route," she replied, her tone clipped. "ETA three minutes."

"Make it faster," I muttered, glancing toward Vitale.

He exchanged a look with the masked figure before nodding. They retreated toward the estate gates, covering their exit with suppressive fire.

"Leo!" I called, signalling for him to pursue.

He nodded, breaking into a sprint as Judie and I provided cover.

Aftermath

The courtyard was littered with the remnants of the firefight—shattered stone, spent casings, and the moans of injured attackers. Vitale and the masked figure had escaped, but we'd captured two of his men, their wounds ensuring they wouldn't resist further interrogation. Ruby appeared at the edge of the courtyard, her face pale but determined.

"Are you okay?" she asked, her eyes scanning me for injuries.

"I'm fine," I assured her, though my adrenaline was still spiking. "Vitale got away, but we've got leverage now."

Her gaze flicked to the prisoners, then back to me. "Do you think they'll talk?"

"They will," I said, my voice cold. "Everyone has a breaking point."

As the cleanup began, Leo returned, his expression grim. "They had a car waiting outside the perimeter. We couldn't catch them."

"They're not going far," I said, my mind already racing through the possibilities. "Francesca's bold, but tonight she overplayed her hand. She won't see what's coming next."

Ruby stepped closer, her voice low. "What about Mancini?"
"He's still in the safehouse," I replied. "He'll be our next move."
Her hand brushed mine, grounding me. "Be careful, Ryan. Whatever Francesca's planning, it's bigger than us." I nodded, the weight of her words settling over me. Bigger, yes—but not insurmountable. Because no matter how far Francesca's reach extended, I would find a way to end this. The interrogation room was dimly lit, the flickering fluorescent bulb casting uneasy shadows on the walls. The two men we'd captured sat across from me, their hands bound to the table. They refused to speak, their defiance etched in the tight lines of their faces. Leo loomed behind me, his imposing presence a silent reminder of the consequences of silence. Ruby waited outside, her insistence that she wasn't part of interrogations holding firm. But I could feel her anxiety through the one-way glass; she was watching, piecing things together as we unravelled Francesca's plans. One of the captives shifted in his seat, his restraint beginning to crack. "You don't know who you're dealing with," he spat, his voice laced with venom. I leaned forward, my tone calm but sharp. "Then enlighten me. Tell me who Francesca has aligned herself with." The man smirked, his lip curling like he knew something I didn't. "It's not about who she's aligned with. It's about you. It's always been about you, Giovannetti." The air grew heavier, his words striking a nerve I couldn't fully place.

Leo's hand rested briefly on my shoulder, grounding me, as I pressed further. "What do you mean?"

"You've got skeletons, don't you?" the man said, his grin widening. "Buried so deep even your perfect wife doesn't know. But Francesca... she knows everything."

My jaw clenched as I stood abruptly, the chair scraping against the floor.

"You're running out of time to be useful."

"I'm not afraid of you," he taunted, leaning back in his chair. "But maybe she should be."

I slammed my hands on the table, the sound echoing in the room. "Enough games. Talk, or I swear you'll regret it."

Before I could push further, Mia's voice crackled through the comms. "Ryan, we've got an update. Mancini's requesting a meeting—says he has information you need." I exhaled sharply, turning toward Leo. "Secure them. We're not done here."

The Revelation

The safehouse was cloaked in an eerie silence when Ruby and I arrived. Mancini sat in the corner, his injuries treated but his eyes alert and calculating. He didn't flinch as I approached, his smirk a shadow of his usual bravado.

"You wanted to talk?" I asked, my tone icy.

Mancini nodded, his gaze flicking briefly to Ruby. "It's not you I wanted to see. It's her." Ruby stiffened beside me, her eyes narrowing. "If you have something to say, say it." Mancini chuckled darkly, leaning forward. "Does he know that you're stronger than he thinks? That you'll walk away the moment you see the truth?"

"Enough," I snapped, but Mancini ignored me.

"Francesca has a gift for digging up the past," he continued, his voice dripping with malice. "And Ryan's past is... colourful."

Ruby's eyes flicked to me, confusion and a hint of fear surfacing. "What's he talking about, Ryan?"

"It's nothing," I said quickly, my voice firmer than I intended. "He's trying to manipulate us."

Mancini's laugh was low and cruel. "You think you can bury it forever? Secrets have a way of clawing their way to the surface." I stepped closer to him, my temper fraying. "You don't know what you're talking about."

"Don't I?" Mancini shot back. "Tell her, Ryan. Tell her who really started the fire that burned the Vitale estate all those years ago killing his whole family."

Ruby's breath hitched, her hand gripping my arm as her eyes widened. "What is he saying?"

"It's a lie," I said firmly, my gaze locked on Mancini. "He's trying to divide us."

But doubt flickered in Ruby's eyes, and I felt the ground shift beneath me. "Ryan... you told me it was an accident. That it wasn't you." I hesitated for a fraction of a second too long. Mancini caught it, and his grin widened. "Oh, it wasn't an accident. He lit the match himself, darling. All for revenge." Ruby stepped back, her hand slipping from my arm as she stared at me. "Is that true?" I swallowed hard, forcing myself to meet her gaze. "Ruby, it's not what you think—"

"Is. It. True?" Her voice was cold now, cutting through the fragile silence between us.

The weight of my past crashed over me, the truth clawing its way out despite my efforts to bury it. "I didn't mean for it to happen like that," I admitted, my voice low. "It was supposed to be a message. Not... not what it became." Her expression fractured, pain and betrayal warring in her eyes. "You lied to me. After everything, you lied."

"I was trying to protect you," I said desperately. "I didn't want you to see that side of me."

"You should have trusted me," she said, her voice breaking. "Instead, you let me believe you were someone you're not."

I reached for her, but she stepped back, her eyes filling with tears she refused to let fall. "Ruby, please—"

"Don't," she whispered, her hands trembling. "I need time. To think. To figure out if I can trust you again."

Her words gutted me, but I nodded, understanding the gravity of what I'd done. As she walked away, Mancini's voice broke the silence.
"She's not like us, Ryan. She doesn't belong in this world."
I turned to him, my fury barely contained. "Shut up." He smirked, leaning back. "You'll see. She'll leave you, and when she does, you'll realize that we're all you have left." I slammed the door on his laughter, but the damage was done.

Heart of the Storm

The air felt thick with tension as I walked through the hallways of the estate, my footsteps echoing in the silence. Every inch of me was on edge, but the weight of the past—my past—was pulling me down like an anchor. Ruby's face, her pain, the doubt in her eyes—it tore at me. I had lied to her, buried truths that had never been meant for her, but now they were out in the open, and I didn't know how to fix it. I found her standing by the window, staring out over the estate's grounds. The storm was rolling in, dark clouds swallowing the sky. The air crackled with the promise of rain. Ruby didn't turn as I approached, her gaze fixed on the horizon, distant.

> "I didn't know how to tell you," I said, my voice quiet, as if speaking too loudly would shatter the fragile moment. "It was... a different time, Ruby. I thought I could bury it, thought it wouldn't affect you."

Her shoulders tensed, but she didn't look at me. "You should've trusted me."

> "I was trying to protect you," I insisted, my hands outstretched as if to reach for her, to pull her back toward me. "I never wanted you to see that side of me."

"But I *did*," she said, her voice barely a whisper, the weight of her words heavier than any accusation. "And now I can't unsee it, Ryan. I can't pretend it didn't happen. I trusted you with everything, and you *lied*."

The storm outside raged on, the wind howling against the windows, mirroring the tempest inside me. "I know I hurt you. But what you need to understand is, I didn't do it for me—I did it for us. For *this*. For what we've built." Ruby turned then, her eyes glistening with unshed tears, but there was no anger in her expression—only a deep, quiet sadness. "How can I believe that when you've kept so many secrets from me? How do I know what's real anymore?" I took a step forward, desperate to reach her, but I could feel the distance between us growing, pulling tighter with each word. "Ruby, please. I never wanted this for us. I never wanted the past to catch up with us."

"You should have been honest," she repeated, her voice steady despite the pain. "I would've understood. You don't have to hide from me. You never had to."

The air between us grew colder, as if the storm outside was seeping into the very heart of the estate. The storm wasn't just in the sky—it was in us, in every word that we hadn't said, in every secret I'd kept buried for too long. And as much as I wanted to fix it, I didn't know if I could. Ruby stepped back, her arms crossing over her chest like a shield, creating an invisible wall between us. "I don't know if I can keep doing this," she said softly. "I don't know if I can keep loving someone who's always hiding pieces of themselves from me."

"No—Ruby, please," I begged, my heart racing in my chest. "I love you. I *need* you. You're the only thing that keeps me from falling apart."

She shook her head, her voice barely audible, over the sound of the rain pounding against the windows. "I don't know if that's enough anymore, Ryan."

The words hit me like a physical blow. I had no answer, nothing to say that could make the pain go away, because in that moment, I realized the truth: I had hurt her, irreparably, and now I was paying the price. But I couldn't lose her. I couldn't let everything we'd built together—our love, our future—crumble because of the past. As if sensing my inner turmoil, Ruby looked back out the window, her breath fogging up the glass. "I need time," she said, her voice quiet but resolute. "I need time to figure out if I can forgive you."

"Ruby, I'll do anything," I said, my voice thick with emotion.
"I'll give you the time. But please don't give up on us."

She didn't respond immediately, and I watched helplessly as she stood there, the storm outside blurring the line between sky and earth, just as the storm inside our hearts blurred the line between love and betrayal.

Hours passed, but I couldn't shake the weight of her words. I found myself pacing through the halls, my mind racing. What could I do? What could I say to prove to her that she was the only thing that mattered to me, that I would sacrifice anything—everything—to make things right? As the night dragged on, the storm outside intensified, the thunder cracking like a whip against the sky. But the real storm was inside—inside me, inside Ruby. I could feel her distance growing with every passing second, every moment I wasn't there to hold her, to make things right. Finally, after what felt like an eternity, I stood outside her door, my hand resting on the cold handle. I hesitated for a long moment, my pulse pounding in my ears. She needed space, but how could I give her space when every second away from her felt like I was losing her? I knocked softly, my heart in my throat.

"Ruby?"

For a long moment, there was nothing but silence. And then, just as I was about to turn away, the door creaked open, and she stood there—her face drawn, her eyes swollen from the tears she hadn't let fall in front of me.

"I'm sorry," she said, her voice barely above a whisper.

"I know," I replied, my voice hoarse. "But I won't stop trying. I won't stop trying to fix this."

Ruby stepped aside, letting me in, and for the first time in hours, the world felt like it might not be falling apart. But the truth hung in the air between us like a storm cloud, dark and threatening, waiting to break.

"I need to know who you are, Ryan," she said quietly, her eyes searching mine. "I need to know if I can trust the man standing in front of me."

I nodded, my throat tight. "I'll show you. I'll prove it to you, every day." Her eyes softened just a fraction, but the doubt was still there. "I want to believe you. But I can't just forget what you've done."

"I know," I said, my voice barely a whisper. "But I'll make it right. I'll show you I'm worth trusting."

And as the rain pounded outside, I realized the storm wasn't just in the world around us—it was in us. The question now was whether we could weather it together, or if the storm would tear us apart. The hours that followed were a blur. Time seemed to slow, each minute stretching out like a tightrope I was walking on, uncertain whether I'd reach the other side. Ruby remained quiet, her gaze distant as she sat across from me. Her presence felt both comforting and painful. The love between us was still there, but it was buried beneath layers of distrust, the foundation of our relationship cracked by the revelations I had kept hidden for so long.

The storm outside raged on, but it was the storm within me that demanded my attention. I couldn't let this break us. I couldn't let the man I once was, the mistakes I made, destroy everything Ruby and I had fought so hard to build. Ruby finally broke the silence, her voice softer than I'd expected. "I don't know if I can do this, Ryan. I don't know if I can go on trusting you when I feel like I barely know who you are anymore." I clenched my fists, the weight of her words threatening to suffocate me. "I'm sorry. I wish I could go back and change it all. I never wanted to keep these things from you, but I thought I was protecting you. I thought if you knew, it would ruin everything."

Ruby shook her head, her fingers tracing absent circles on the table between us. "You think that by hiding the truth, you're protecting me? By keeping your secrets, you're only hurting me more. I need you to be honest with me, Ryan—about everything. No more lies." Her words cut through me like a blade. I had spent so long protecting my past, keeping the darkness at bay, but now it was all spilling out, and I couldn't stop it. I took a deep breath, gathering the courage I had been avoiding. "There's more you don't know. More that I haven't told you." Ruby's eyes locked onto mine, her expression unreadable. "I'm listening." For a long moment, I didn't speak. My mind raced, torn between the urge to shield her from the truth and the undeniable need to come clean. I had to. For her—for us.

> "I'm not the man you think I am," I began, my voice strained. "Before you, before everything we built together, I made choices. Choices I regret, choices that changed everything. But there's one thing I never told you—one thing that's been eating away at me since we first met."

Ruby's gaze hardened, her eyes searching mine as if trying to see beyond the words. "What is it?"

I hesitated, the weight of the confession choking me. "Alessandro Vitale—he's not just some businessman. He's someone I used to work with. He was a part of everything—my past, the people I trusted, the people I betrayed. But it wasn't just him. There were others, people like Giovanni Mancini, Francesca D'Alessandro... and Dante Romano. They were all connected, tied to the things I did." Ruby's face paled, her lips trembling as the truth settled in. I could see the realization creeping into her eyes. She had suspected pieces of this, but now it was all laid bare.

"I was involved in things, Ruby," I continued, my voice faltering. "Things I thought I could escape. I thought I could outrun them. But you can't outrun your past. You can't outrun the people who will use anything against you—your weaknesses, your mistakes, your family. It's all connected, and they won't stop until they've taken everything from us."

Ruby stood up abruptly, pacing back and forth, her mind racing just as mine had been. "You... you were involved with them? All this time?"

"I didn't want you to know," I said quickly, my hands outstretched, trying to close the distance between us. "I thought if I kept it hidden, I could protect you from it. But I see now—I was wrong. I should've trusted you. I should've let you in."

She stopped, her back to me, her breath ragged as she fought to contain the storm within her. "You don't get it, Ryan," she whispered, her voice breaking. "It's not just the secrets. It's everything. It's the way you've built this life, this... *us*, on lies. You don't trust me with your past, with the worst parts of you. How can I trust you with my future?" I closed the distance between us, gently turning her toward me. "I never meant to hurt you. I never meant to make you feel like you weren't enough. You *are* enough, Ruby. You've always been enough. And if you'll let me, I'll show you—every day, with every choice I make from now on." Ruby's eyes filled with tears, but she didn't pull away. "I want to believe you. I do. But you've given me so many reasons not to." The truth hung heavy in the air, as if the storm outside had crawled into the very room with us. The silence between us was a cold thing, full of questions with no answers, doubts with no resolution. The distance between us was widening with every unspoken word, and I could feel it—the fragile thread that had held us together for so long was unravelling.

> "I need to know if you can forgive me," I said quietly, my voice low, filled with a raw desperation I couldn't mask. "If you can forgive *us*. Because I can't lose you, Ruby. I can't."

Ruby's hands trembled at her sides, and for a moment, I thought she might pull away. But instead, she looked up at me, her gaze softer than it had been moments before. "I don't know, Ryan. I don't know if I can forgive everything. But I'll try. I will." The words felt like a lifeline, a fragile promise amid the storm. I reached out, gently cupping her cheek, the warmth of her skin grounding me in the chaos.

> "We'll get through this," I said, my voice thick with emotion. "Together."

The rain outside began to subside, the thunder fading, but the storm between us was far from over. It would take time, and patience, and the will to face the truth—even the ugly truths we hadn't wanted to confront. But if we were together, I knew we had a chance. A chance to rebuild, to trust again. We weren't out of the storm yet—but I would fight for us, for our future. No matter what it took. The quiet that followed felt suffocating, a silence that pressed in from all sides.

Ruby stood there, her body tense, her breath shallow as she processed everything, I had told her. I didn't know if it was the truth that hurt the most, or the fact that I had kept it hidden from her for so long. I had always thought I was protecting her, but now I saw it clearly—by hiding my past, I had made us both prisoners of my mistakes. She finally spoke, her voice barely above a whisper. "How could you think I wouldn't want to know? You've always said we were partners in this—partners in everything. Why didn't you trust me with this?"

"I thought I could protect you from the darkness in my past," I said, my voice raw. "But I see now—I was wrong. I should have trusted you. I should've trusted us."

Ruby wiped her eyes with the back of her hand, a shaky breath escaping her lips. "You've kept me in the dark, Ryan. All this time, you've kept me at arm's length, and now I don't even know who you are anymore." The weight of her words hit me like a physical blow. I knew I had hurt her. I could see it in the way she stood, distant and torn, like she was looking at a stranger. I wanted to take it all back, to find a way to fix this, but I couldn't change what had already been done. The truth was out, and now we had to find a way to rebuild, if it was even possible. I took a step toward her, my heart pounding. "I'm not the man I was, Ruby. You've changed me. You gave me a reason to fight for something better. But I've made mistakes. I've hurt you, and I don't expect you to forgive me right away. I just need you to know that I'll spend the rest of my life making it right. I'm not running from this anymore."

Ruby didn't answer right away. She turned, walking to the window, her back to me as she stared out at the storm still raging beyond the glass. I could hear the faint rumble of thunder in the distance, but it felt like a distant echo compared to the storm inside the walls of our home.

The silence stretched on, and I could feel myself unravelling, my every instinct telling me to fix this, to do anything I could to make things right. But the truth was, I had no idea if I could fix this. No matter how much I loved her, the damage I had done might be too much to overcome. Finally, Ruby spoke, her voice low but steady. "I want to believe you, Ryan. I really do. But you've lied to me for so long, kept things from me... How can I know if I can trust you again?" I stepped forward, my voice firm but filled with vulnerability. "I won't lie to you again, Ruby. I swear. You're my priority now. Everything else... everything else comes second. If you'll let me, I'll prove it. Every day." She turned to face me then, her eyes still filled with uncertainty, but there was something else there too—a flicker of hope, or maybe just the barest trace of it. "I don't know what to do, Ryan. I don't know if I can just forget everything. But... I'm willing to try. I'm willing to try if you're ready to show me that this—us—is worth fighting for."

I nodded, my chest tight with the weight of her words. "I'm ready. I've been ready for a long time. I won't stop fighting, Ruby. Not for us." Ruby looked at me for a long moment, her gaze searching, weighing the words I had spoken, measuring their sincerity. Slowly, she nodded. It wasn't an affirmation, not yet. But it was a start. A fragile, uncertain start, but a start all the same.

"I hope you mean that, Ryan. I really do."

"I do." The words were steady now, because I knew they were true. "I do."

The rain continued to beat against the windows, the thunder now distant, as if the storm outside was beginning to subside. But I knew this was just the calm before the real storm. The storm that would rage within us, testing our trust, our commitment, and everything we had built together.

Ruby stepped toward me, closing the distance between us. Her hand reached out, gently cupping my face, her thumb brushing over my cheek in a silent gesture that spoke louder than any words could. There was still so much between us—so many unspoken fears and doubts—but in that moment, I could feel a flicker of something familiar. A trace of the love that had always been there, waiting, buried beneath the hurt.

"I need time," Ruby whispered, her voice quiet but resolute. "I need time to process everything, Ryan. This isn't something that gets fixed overnight."

"I know," I said, my voice thick with emotion. "I'm not asking for everything to be fixed right now. I just want the chance to show you that I can be the man you need me to be."

She nodded, her hand slipping away from my face. "Okay. But I need you to be patient with me. I need time to figure out if I can trust you again." I took a deep breath, my heart pounding in my chest. "I'll wait for as long as it takes." Ruby's eyes softened, and for the first time in what felt like an eternity, there was a flicker of hope. A tiny crack in the wall that had grown between us, and maybe—just maybe—if I was patient enough, we could rebuild.

"We'll get through this," I said, reaching out to gently take her hand in mine. "Together."

She didn't pull away, and that was enough—for now. Together, we would face the storm, whatever it took. Because love, even fractured, was worth fighting for. And as the rain finally began to ease, I held onto that truth with everything I had. The days following that conversation were marked by a quiet tension. Ruby and I coexisted in a fragile truce, moving through the motions of our daily lives, each of us retreating into our own thoughts, trying to come to terms with the weight of everything that had happened. There were moments where I could almost convince myself that things were returning to normal—that the love we shared was enough to overcome this storm. But then the cracks would appear again, and I'd be reminded of how much we'd lost in those few moments of truth. Ruby still wasn't the same. She smiled, but it didn't quite reach her eyes. She still held my hand at times, but there was a wariness in the way her fingers hesitated before intertwining with mine. I knew she was trying, but I also knew that the road back to what we had was not going to be easy. And I wasn't sure if I could get us there. I couldn't erase my past, but I was determined to prove that the man I was becoming was worthy of her trust, of her love. Ruby was in the kitchen when I walked in that morning, her back to me as she carefully measured out ingredients for breakfast. The smell of fresh coffee filled the air, mingling with the faint scent of vanilla. I stood in the doorway, watching her for a moment before stepping forward, closing the distance between us.

"Morning," I said, my voice quieter than usual, as if testing the waters.

Ruby didn't turn around immediately, but I saw her hand pause for a moment before she placed the measuring cup down. "Morning," she replied, her voice soft but strained.

"I—" I stopped myself, unsure of how to proceed.

I could feel the weight of everything still hanging between us, like a rope pulled taut and threatening to snap. She sighed, turning to face me, her expression unreadable. "Ryan, we can't keep pretending that things are normal." I nodded, swallowing the lump that had formed in my throat. "I know."

"I'm trying," Ruby said, her voice barely above a whisper. "I want to trust you again, but I don't know if I can just forget everything..."

"I don't want you to forget," I said quickly, my heart racing. "I just want you to know that I'm here. For whatever it takes. I'm not going anywhere. I'll prove that to you. Every single day."

Her gaze softened just slightly, but there was still that uncertainty in her eyes—the same uncertainty that had been there since I'd revealed the truth. It was like a shadow that wouldn't leave her, no matter how hard she tried to push it away.

"I need you to understand," Ruby continued, her voice trembling now. "I don't know if I can ever fully trust you the way I did before. That's not something that just comes back."

The words hit me harder than I expected, and I could feel the sting deep inside. I nodded, trying to keep my emotions in check. "I understand," I said quietly. "I don't expect everything to be fixed overnight. Just... don't give up on me, Ruby. I know I've messed up, but I'll spend the rest of my life making it right." Ruby took a deep breath, her shoulders tense as she let out a slow exhale. "I'm not giving up on us, Ryan. But you have to give me time. I need time."

"I'll give you all the time you need," I said, my voice steady, despite the storm raging inside of me. "I'll wait. Just don't shut me out. We'll figure this out together."

Her eyes searched mine for a long moment before she finally nodded. There was still a trace of pain in her expression, but something had shifted. Maybe it was the smallest glimmer of hope, or maybe it was just the realization that we were both trying.

Ruby stepped toward me, her hand reaching out to touch my arm, the gesture hesitant but genuine. "I'm not asking you to change overnight, Ryan. I'm just asking for honesty—for us to be honest with each other, even when it's hard." I gently cupped her face in my hands, brushing my thumb along her cheek, feeling the warmth of her skin beneath my touch. "I swear, I'll never hide anything from you again. You deserve the truth, Ruby. Always." We stood there for a moment, the silence stretching between us, but it wasn't as heavy as it had been. It was something else—something I couldn't quite place, but something that felt a little more like hope. Finally, Ruby let out a quiet sigh, her body relaxing just slightly as she leaned into my touch. "Okay," she whispered. "We'll take this one step at a time." One step at a time. It wasn't the resolution I had hoped for, but it was a start. And sometimes, a start was all you needed.

The next few days passed in a blur. The storm that had been raging inside of us seemed to settle, just a little, but the world around us refused to slow down. There were still enemies to face, secrets to uncover, and threats lurking in every shadow. But in the quiet moments, when we weren't fighting for our survival, we found ourselves reconnecting. Slowly. Gently. Every conversation was more honest, every touch less guarded. I knew there was still a long way to go, that the path ahead was far from clear, but for the first time in what felt like forever, I believed we could make it through. And as I looked at Ruby one last time before I left for another mission, I knew one thing for certain: whatever happened, I would fight for us. I would fight for her. Together, we would weather the storm.

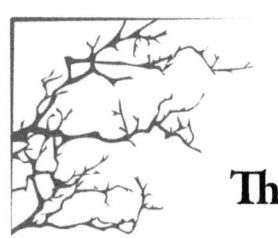

The Longest Night

The estate, once a sanctuary, now felt like a cage. The roar of the helicopters overhead sent tremors through the ground, and the muffled sounds of vehicles approaching signalled the storm closing in on us. I could feel the weight of every second ticking away, each heartbeat louder than the last.

"Elena's dead," I muttered under my breath, the words hitting harder than they should.

I never expected the situation to escalate so quickly—never imagined a quiet betrayal would lead to this. But it had. And now, the full brunt of our enemies was on us, coming at us from every direction. Mia's voice crackled through the comms. "They're here. Multiple vehicles. Armed. Heading toward the estate." I shot a look at Ruby, the urgency in her eyes matching my own. We didn't have time to strategize, no more time for careful moves. Our options were dwindling, and the only one left was to escape.

"We need to move. Now," I said, my voice harsh with resolve.

Leo and the team were already on the move, each of them coordinating to hold off the oncoming forces long enough for Ruby and me to get to safety. But it was clear that this was no longer about a clean getaway. It was about surviving the night. We hurried through the back hallways, my thoughts racing. The attackers weren't just ordinary mercenaries—they had the resources of Vitale, D'Alessandro, and Romano backing them. These were men who had been waiting for a moment like this, knowing that sooner or later we'd slip up, that our past would catch up with us. We reached the side door leading to the gardens. The lush greenery was our only cover, the thick shadows giving us a brief advantage. But even as we pushed through the door and into the night, I knew we were being hunted.

"Where's Leo?" Ruby's voice was tight, her grip on my arm almost frantic.

She was trying to keep it together, but I could feel her anxiety rising.

"He's holding them off," I said, though the words didn't feel reassuring. The sound of footsteps echoed in the distance, getting closer with each passing second. "We don't have much time."

We had no choice but to head toward the back gate, the one exit least likely to be covered. But the closer we got, the more I could feel the tension in the air. I didn't need to look over my shoulder to know they were coming. Suddenly, the sharp sound of gunfire shattered the night. The crack of bullets hitting the stone walls around us sent us diving for cover. My heart pounded in my chest as I pulled Ruby down beside me.

"They're here," I whispered, my voice cold with resolve.

Ruby's hand gripped mine, her fingers shaking, but she didn't let go. She never did.

"Ryan, we can't outrun them. We need to fight," she said, her tone a mix of fear and determination. Her eyes were wide, but there was no hesitation in her voice.

I looked at her, seeing the same fear mirrored in her expression that I was feeling inside. But Ruby had always been my strength. Always.

"We'll fight, but we'll fight smart," I said, trying to calm myself even as adrenaline surged through my veins. "We head for the treeline. It's the only chance we've got."

We made a run for it, staying low as the gunfire continued to rain down around us. Every movement felt like an eternity, every step a heartbeat away from danger. We could hear the helicopters above, the steady hum of their blades growing louder, closer. Mia's voice came through the comms, strained with urgency. "Ryan, Ruby—there's too many of them. They're setting up roadblocks. You need to move fast." We didn't need to be told twice. We had to outrun this. Our lives depended on it. The sound of men shouting echoed from the estate as we sprinted through the garden, pushing through the underbrush toward the treeline. My mind raced with calculations, trying to figure out how much time we had before we were trapped. We reached the edge of the trees, but just as we started to push deeper into the cover, another shot rang out. I heard Ruby gasp as she stumbled, the bullet grazing her shoulder.

"Ruby!" I shouted, spinning to catch her. She winced but didn't fall. Her eyes were fierce, even as she gritted her teeth.

"I'm fine," she said, though her voice was strained. She nodded toward the trees. "We need to move."

I didn't question her. We pushed on, deeper into the woods, the sound of pursuit growing louder behind us. I could hear them shouting, could feel the threat closing in. There was no clear escape route, no guarantee that we'd make it through the night. But all I cared about was getting Ruby to safety. The trees were thick with shadows, but every step felt like we were running out of time. We couldn't keep up this pace forever. My mind raced—there had to be another way.

But just as we cleared the treeline, a pair of headlights flashed through the darkness. The roadblock had been set.

"Ryan, we're trapped!" Ruby gasped, her eyes wide with fear.

I turned toward the sound of the vehicles, my heart hammering. They were here. And they were closing in faster than we'd anticipated. There was no choice now. We had to fight. I pulled Ruby behind a large tree, signalling to the others. "We take them head-on," I said, my voice hard and sure. "This ends tonight." Ruby nodded, her hand in mine, ready for whatever came next. She always was. The night was long. The stakes were higher than they'd ever been before. But we were going to survive it. Together. The air was thick with the scent of earth and gunpowder. My breath came in ragged bursts as we crouched behind the tree, the sound of footsteps and the distant hum of the helicopters drawing closer. The night was growing darker, colder, and I knew we didn't have much time. But then, as I reached for Ruby's hand, a sharp pain erupted in my side. The force of it sent me staggering backward, my legs giving out beneath me as I hit the ground hard.

"Ryan!" Ruby's voice was panicked, her hands reaching for me, but I could already feel the blood soaking through my shirt, the warmth spreading across my chest.

The bullet had entered in my side, and out again without hitting vitals, but it wasn't just the physical pain—it was the realization that we were running out of time.

"Stay down!" Leo's voice crackled in my earpiece. "We've got eyes on you. Hold on, we're coming."

I gritted my teeth, struggling to sit up. "No time," I forced out, my voice rough. "Get Ruby to safety. I'll hold them off."

Ruby's face was pale, her expression caught between fear and fury. She placed a hand on my chest, holding me down. "You're not going anywhere. We stay together. Understand?" I could see the determination in her eyes. There was no arguing with her, not when she was like this. She had always been the one who grounded me, who pulled me back from the edge. The pain was sharp, but I forced it down, pushing myself to my feet. "We move," I said, gritting my teeth. "We have to keep moving." I could feel the pressure in my side where the blood was soaking through my shirt, but there was no time to deal with it. The noise was getting closer—footsteps, gunfire, the low hum of engines. We were running out of options.

"Leo, status?" I hissed into the comms, trying to keep my voice steady despite the blood clouding my thoughts.

"We're still at the perimeter," Leo responded. "But they're closing in. You need to get out of there, now."

I glanced over at Ruby. She was already scanning the area, her instincts sharp. "Head north," she said, pointing into the woods. "There's a trail we can use." I nodded, barely able to catch my breath, but the sharp pain in my side made every movement more difficult. Still, I forced myself to follow Ruby as she led the way through the trees, moving swiftly despite the weight of the situation. The trees thinned as we neared the ridge, the path becoming steeper. My vision swam a little, but I refused to stop. I wasn't going to let this end here.

"We'll make it," Ruby said, her voice steady despite the circumstances, her hand tightening around mine. "We have to."

I nodded, swallowing the blood that was rising in my throat. I wasn't sure how much longer I could go on, but I couldn't show her any weakness—not now. Not when she was putting everything on the line for me. A gunshot rang out, echoing through the trees. I jerked, my heart racing, but it wasn't aimed at us. It was a warning shot, the sound of a vehicle coming to a stop on the ridge behind us.

"Dante," I muttered, my pulse quickening.

Ruby tensed, her eyes searching the darkened woods. "We're running out of time," she said, her voice low, but filled with that same unwavering resolve I'd come to depend on. I couldn't deny it. We had no more options left. Suddenly, a loud crash echoed through the trees, followed by the sound of boots stomping toward us. They were close. Too close. Without thinking, I pulled Ruby down behind a thick cluster of trees, the cold ground beneath us a bitter reminder of how far we'd fallen. My side was screaming, blood leaking from the wound, but I couldn't stop now. There was no time.

"They're here," I whispered, my breath ragged. "They'll push us to the edge. We need to make a stand."

Ruby's hand tightened around mine, her expression fierce. "Not like this. We won't go out like this." I met her gaze, her unwavering strength a lifeline amid the storm. We were running out of time, but I knew one thing for certain—if we were going down, it wouldn't be without a fight. The sound of footsteps grew louder, but just as they closed in on us, the unmistakable sound of gunfire came from behind. Leo and the team had found us.

"Move!" Leo shouted, his voice cutting through the chaos. "Get out of there, now!"

Ruby didn't hesitate. She pulled me up, pushing through the pain in my side. Together, we sprinted toward the thick trees where Leo and the team were waiting, the sound of gunfire now a constant buzz in the air.

We weren't safe yet. But at least, for now, we were still alive. The woods felt endless as we ran, the cold air biting at my skin, mingling with the sharp pain in my side. Every breath I took felt like I was breathing fire, the wound in my side a constant reminder that we were in the thick of it. The adrenaline was a haze, but it kept me moving, kept me alive. Ruby's hand gripped mine, her steps steady, even though

I could feel the weight of her uncertainty, her hesitation. I could feel her eyes on me, even when I wasn't looking at her. The mistrust that had lingered between us since the truth of my past came to light, it still hung there, thick and unspoken. She was still grappling with the lie I'd told her—the part of me I'd buried so deep it almost didn't seem real anymore. And even now, when we were running for our lives, when everything depended on us sticking together, I could still feel that distance in her touch.

But something had shifted, and I could see it in the way she moved. The way she held my hand. It wasn't just the instinct to survive, not just the fight to make it through the night. It was something deeper—something that said, despite everything, she was still here. She was still trusting me, even if just a little. Even though the weight of my past still had its hold on her heart. We were running—no, we were *surviving*—and Ruby was still with me. And that was enough.

> "Ryan," Ruby's voice broke through the haze, sharp, filled with an urgency that made me turn my head toward her. "We need to keep moving."

But before I could respond, the sharp *crack* of gunfire echoed through the trees. I didn't even hear it coming, but I felt it.

Another bullet—this one slamming into my back. The force of it knocked me forward, and I gasped, the air rushing out of me as the pain hit like a freight train.

"Ryan!" Ruby screamed, but I barely registered her words.

The pain was blinding, my legs nearly giving out beneath me as I stumbled forward, my body on fire.

> "Keep moving!" I forced out through gritted teeth, my voice ragged.

The bullet wasn't fatal, but it was damn close. I could feel the blood seeping out, the warmth spreading across my back, but I couldn't stop. Not now. Ruby's grip on me tightened, and she steadied me, pulling me along as we ran for our lives. Her eyes were wide, panicked—but her strength was still there, still holding me together.

> "I'm not leaving you," Ruby said, her voice filled with determination, though the tremor in her hands betrayed her. The same hands that were helping me stay upright, keeping me on my feet. "We're getting out of this."

I could feel the warmth of her hand, the way she was holding me close. The weight of her doubt still lingered, but in that moment, there was no room for it. We were here, together. And I was going to keep fighting, for her, for us. Another round of gunfire rang out, closer this time. I could hear the thudding of boots on the ground behind us, but we had no choice. We had to push forward. I pulled Ruby closer, my mind racing through the endless scenarios of what could happen next. We had to keep moving.

> "Leo," I called through the comms, my voice low, barely audible over the sound of our hurried steps. "Where are you?"

> "We're on the north side," Leo's voice crackled back. "I'm tracking your position. Hold on—we're almost there."

I gritted my teeth as we stumbled forward, Ruby's arm wrapped around my waist to support me. We were getting close to the ridge, but the gunfire was growing louder, more intense. My breathing was laboured, my vision blurry from the pain and the blood loss. But then something in Ruby's eyes shifted. I could see it—her resolve. The mistrust, the doubt, it was still there, but beneath it, there was something more. Something that told me she was with me, no matter the cost. She had always been strong. But now, she was trusting me—*trusting us*. Ruby squeezed my hand tighter. "We're getting through this. Together."

In that moment, I felt it—the weight of the lie I'd told her, the distance it had caused between us, but also the truth of this moment. Right now, nothing else mattered. We were in this together, and we'd make it out alive. No matter the cost. Another gunshot rang out, this time ricocheting off a nearby tree, but I was focused on one thing: getting to safety. We didn't stop, not for a second, not until we were through the trees and in the clearing where Leo and the team were waiting, weapons raised, ready for whatever was coming next. But Ruby was still beside me, holding me steady. No matter the dangers, the past, or the betrayals that had led us here, she was still with me. And that meant everything. We barely made it to the clearing, the shadows of the trees swallowing us whole as we stumbled through the underbrush. I could hear the snap of twigs behind us, the echo of heavy boots growing closer. The urgency in Ruby's grip on my arm never wavered, her strength carrying us both forward even as I struggled to stay upright.

> "Stay with me, Ryan," she murmured through clenched teeth, her face tense with worry. The pain from the bullet wounds in my back and side was starting to dull with each step, but my body was running on fumes, the adrenaline wearing off and leaving behind a haze of exhaustion.

I leaned into her, not wanting to burden her further but knowing I had no choice. My breathing was laboured, and I could taste the bitterness of blood in my mouth, but there was a fire in Ruby's eyes—a quiet resolve that told me we weren't done yet.

"Leo?" I rasped into the comms again, my voice strained.

"Hold tight," Leo's voice crackled, sharper this time, urgent. "We're on our way."

The night seemed to stretch endlessly, the air thick with the scent of earth and the sharp sting of gunpowder still hanging in the air. But I couldn't afford to focus on that. I had to keep my head, keep my eyes on the horizon. There was no time for second thoughts. Suddenly, a flash of movement caught my eye. A figure appeared at the edge of the clearing, stepping out from behind a cluster of trees. At first, I thought it was one of my team, but then I saw the glint of steel in their hand, and I realized that wasn't the case.

"Get down!" Ruby shouted, pulling me toward the ground with a force that sent us both tumbling into the brush.

I hit the ground hard, the pain in my back flaring up, but Ruby's quick reflexes saved us from being exposed. A volley of bullets tore through the air, the sound of them whizzing past us too close for comfort.

"Sniper!" Leo's voice came through the comms, just as another round cracked through the air.

I could hear the screech of metal against tree bark, the bullet grazing the edge of my jacket.

Ruby's hand tightened around mine, and I could feel her pulse racing. "We need to move, Ryan," she whispered urgently. "Now." I nodded, gritting my teeth against the pain. We had no choice. We couldn't stay pinned down. Ruby and I scrambled to our feet, moving quickly but cautiously, staying low to the ground. The clearing was open, and the sniper had a clear line of sight, but Leo's team was closing in, moving in from the opposite side. The air crackled with tension, and I could hear the familiar sound of footsteps crunching through the brush. Through the haze of pain, I heard Leo's voice again. "We're almost there! Keep moving!" But I knew that it wasn't going to be that easy. The sniper had a clear shot, and we were too exposed. We needed cover, and fast.

"Ruby," I gasped, my voice barely audibles over the chaos. "I need you to trust me."

Ruby shot me a glance, her eyes flicking over the trees, calculating, analysing. "What are you planning?" I didn't have time for a full explanation. "We need to split up. Draw their fire. I'll circle back around—"

"No," Ruby interrupted, her voice sharp. "I'm not letting you out of my sight, Ryan."

Her words, as firm as they were, sent a strange warmth through me. Despite everything, despite the lies and the betrayals, we were still a team. But the situation was dire, and we needed to move quickly. "Ruby, please," I said, my voice strained. "I can't keep running like this. I need you to give me a chance to flank. It's our best shot." Ruby hesitated, her gaze flicking between me and the shadowy edge of the clearing where the sniper's position must be. For a moment, the world seemed to stop. Then, finally, she nodded, her face tight with determination.

"Don't get yourself killed," she said, her voice low, almost a warning.

"I won't," I promised, though I wasn't sure if I believed myself.

With a last squeeze of her hand, we broke apart. I staggered toward the far side of the clearing, my steps unsteady, my back throbbing with each movement. The sniper's attention was on Ruby now, and I saw the flash of movement as she darted into the trees. I used the cover of darkness to slip into the opposite side, moving as silently as I could, my hand on the grip of my sidearm. The tension in the air was palpable. Time was running out.

I could see the sniper now, crouched on the far ridge, his rifle aimed at Ruby's retreating figure. I took a deep breath and steadied my aim. With a swift motion, I took the shot. The sniper's body jerked, a strangled cry escaping their lips as they fell to the ground, motionless. But there was no time to Savor the moment. I heard heavy boots approaching, shouting from Leo's team as they closed in on the remaining enemy forces. Ruby emerged from the trees, her face pale, but determined. "Ryan are you—" But before she could finish her sentence, there was a new sound—something even worse than gunfire: the roar of an engine. Another vehicle was pulling into the clearing.

"We've got company," I muttered, my body heavy with exhaustion. "And it's not just Leo's team."

Ruby didn't need to ask who it was. She knew. Our night wasn't over. The enemy was closing in, but this time, we wouldn't run. Not anymore. The air was thick with gunfire, and the world seemed to narrow to nothing but the sounds of chaos around us. Every step was a gamble, and every breath a battle. I could feel the blood soaking through my shirt, the pressure of it pooling in my side and back, but there was no time to care about that now. Ruby was down in the brush, low and hidden, but her eyes never left me, a mix of fear and determination etched on her face. She didn't have a weapon, but she was no stranger to danger—she knew what to do.

"Stay down, Ruby," I rasped, though I wasn't sure she could hear me over the roar of the fight.

I gritted my teeth and fired, watching as one of the enemy soldiers dropped to the ground. My vision swam, and my movements were sluggish from blood loss, but the adrenaline kept me moving. The sounds of gunfire echoed through the night as Leo and his team reached us, moving quickly through the dense brush.

"Ryan!" Leo shouted, his voice cutting through the cacophony. "We've got your back!"

I barely nodded before I fired again, the bullet catching an enemy soldier in the shoulder. But there were too many of them, and they were pushing forward with reckless abandon. Leo and his team took their positions with precision, returning fire in a coordinated assault. The gun battle raged on, fierce and unrelenting. The sound of bullets whizzing by was a constant, but I couldn't afford to flinch. Not now. We fought tooth and nail, taking down as many of them as we could. My body felt heavier with each passing minute, the blood loss making it harder to stay upright. But I pushed through. For Ruby. For us. A loud crash to my left made me spin around, aiming my rifle at the new threat. A group of attackers had flanked us, but Leo was already on them, cutting them down with expert precision. The air was thick with smoke and the sharp tang of gunpowder. I could hear men yelling, shouting commands, but they were getting more distant. Fewer of them left.

I stood next to Leo, my rifle steady in my hands, despite the weakness in my body. The enemy was retreating, but they weren't gone yet. Not until we made sure they were.

"Ryan, stay low!" Leo ordered, firing a round into the chest of one last enemy soldier who had been trying to circle around us.

I wasn't listening. My legs were shaking, my vision blurred, but there was no time for weakness. There would be time for that later—if we survived. Another shot rang out, and I turned, instinctively moving to cover Leo, but the bullet caught me in the chest, the impact sending me stumbling backwards. My body gave out, and I dropped to the ground hard, the pain in my side, back and my chest blinding me.

"Ryan!" Ruby's voice was frantic, piercing through the smoke and the gunfire.

I heard her rushing toward me, her footsteps frantic, but I could barely keep my eyes open. The world was spinning. I heard Leo shout something, but it was muffled in my ears. All I could hear now was the pounding of my heart in my chest, slow and steady as I fought to stay conscious. I could feel the blood spreading, soaking through my clothes, pooling beneath me. Through the haze, I saw Ruby's face, fear and determination in her eyes as she knelt beside me, her hands frantic on my chest, trying to stem the flow of blood.

"Stay with me, Ryan," she whispered, her voice trembling, but her touch was steady. "Please, stay with me."

I wanted to tell her I was fine, that I would be okay, but the words wouldn't come. Everything was fading, my body no longer responding as I fought to stay conscious.

The world around me was slipping away, and just before everything went black, I heard Leo yelling: "They are retreating", the last sound before the darkness claimed me, the blood loss and the pain too much to fight any longer...

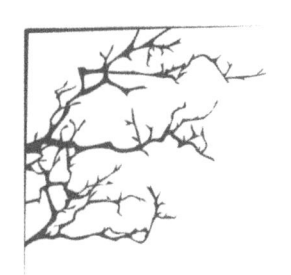

Into the Fire

Pain radiated through every nerve as I struggled to open my eyes. The weight in my chest made it feel like breathing was a battle I was losing. My mind was sluggish, memories swirling of the brutal firefight in the dark brush, the shouting, the adrenaline—and the bullets.

"Ryan, stay with me!" Ruby's voice echoed in my head, frantic and raw, pulling me back to the present.

I blinked against the harsh lights above, realizing I was lying on a medical table, wires and IVs attached to me. The sterile smell of antiseptic was a sharp contrast to the iron tang of blood still lingering in my mind.

"Ryan..." Ruby's voice, softer now, came from beside me.

Her hand was on mine, her fingers trembling. I turned my head to see her sitting close, her eyes rimmed red from tears. I tried to speak, but my throat felt like sandpaper. Finally, I rasped, "You're here..."

"Of course I'm here," she said, her voice breaking. "You think I'd leave you after... after that?"

Her eyes flicked down to my chest, and I followed her gaze. Bandages covered my side, back, and chest—the places where the bullets had struck.

"They said you wouldn't make it," Ruby continued, her voice shaking. "But I told them you're too damn stubborn to die on me."

Her attempt at a smile faltered, and I could see the fear still etched into her features.

"How long?" I croaked.

"Six hours," she replied. "You've been in and out. The docs... they had to stop a lot of bleeding. The chest wound—" She stopped, her throat tightening. "They almost lost you."

I squeezed her hand weakly, trying to ground her—and myself. "I'm still here," I said, though it hurt to form the words.

"Barely," Ruby shot back, her tone laced with anger and fear. "You think this is okay? Charging into gunfire, bleeding out in the middle of nowhere? Ryan, I—" She stopped herself, taking a deep breath.

Her silence hung heavy between us, and I knew it wasn't just fear of losing me that was eating at her.

"Ruby..." I started, but she shook her head.

"Don't," she said, her voice strained. "Not right now. Not after everything."

I swallowed hard, the guilt weighing on me as much as the pain. She was still grappling with the lies I'd told her, the pieces of my past I'd hidden. I wanted to fix it, to explain, but the words felt stuck in my throat.

Before I could say anything, the door opened, and Leo stepped in. His face was a mask of grim determination, but I could see the relief in his eyes when he saw me awake.

"Glad to see you're not dead," he said gruffly. "Because we've got a problem."

"Dante?" I asked, forcing myself to sit up despite Ruby's protests.

Leo nodded. "We intercepted comms. He's regrouping. And this time, he's bringing more firepower." My jaw tightened, anger burning through the haze of pain. "Then we hit him first."

"Ryan, you can't even stand without—" Ruby started, but I cut her off.

"I'm not sitting this out," I said firmly. "This ends now."

Ruby stared at me, her expression a mixture of frustration and something deeper—something that made my chest ache more than the bullet wound ever could.

"Leo," I said, turning to him. "What's the play?"

Leo hesitated, glancing at Ruby before answering. "We've got intel on one of Dante's strongholds. Mancini's been talking, and he's willing to trade more details for protection. But if we're going after Dante, it's going to be all or nothing."

I nodded, ignoring the throbbing pain in my chest. "Then let's go."

"Ryan—" Ruby began, her voice sharp.

"Ruby," I said, meeting her gaze. "I need you to trust me."

She hesitated, her eyes searching mine. "You've lied to me, Ryan. You've kept things from me. And I'm still trying to figure out if I can trust you again, and to top that, you have been shot three times! Just six hours ago!" Her words cut deeper than any bullet, but I held her gaze, my voice steady. "Then let me prove it to you. Let me show you that I'll do whatever it takes to make this right. For us." Ruby's expression softened, though the conflict in her eyes remained. Finally, she nodded. "Fine. But if you pull another stunt like last night, I swear I'll—"

"Noted," I said, managing a faint smile.

Leo cleared his throat, breaking the tension. "If you two are done, we've got work to do." As we prepared to move out, I felt Ruby's hand on my arm. "Just... don't get yourself killed, okay?"

"I'll try," I said, my voice low. "But no promises."

The road ahead was steep, and the fire was closing in. But I wasn't about to let Dante—or my past—destroy everything I'd fought to protect. Not without a fight. The ride to Dante's stronghold was tense, the air in the SUV thick with unspoken words. Ruby sat beside me, her arms crossed, staring out the window. I could feel the weight of her conflicted thoughts pressing down on both of us. Leo drove in silence, his focus on the road, while Judie sat in the front seat, her fingers tapping nervously on the armrest. Mancini had provided a layout of the stronghold—a remote villa surrounded by dense forest, fortified but not impenetrable. He'd also confirmed what we feared: Dante was preparing for an all-out assault on the estate, amassing allies from every corner of his dark empire. If we didn't stop him now, we might not get another chance.

I shifted in my seat, the pain from my wounds a constant reminder of how close I'd come to death. Ruby noticed and glanced at me, her frown deepening.

"You shouldn't be here," she said quietly, her voice tinged with worry.

I met her gaze. "If I'm not here, this doesn't end. You know that." She didn't respond, but the tension in her shoulders told me everything I needed to know. As the villa came into view, Leo slowed the vehicle, pulling off the road into the cover of the trees. We disembarked quickly, moving silently through the underbrush. The moonlight filtering through the branches cast eerie shadows across the forest floor.

"Eyes up," Leo murmured, his rifle at the ready.

We approached the perimeter, crouching behind a low wall. Two guards stood at the main gate, their post illuminated by floodlights. Judie signalled to Mia through the comms.

"Do we have a clear read on the guards?" Judie whispered.

Mia's voice crackled softly in our earpieces. "Two by the gate, three on the balcony overlooking the courtyard. No sign of Dante yet, but he's here. Cameras picked him up an hour ago." Leo turned to me, his expression grim. "We take out the guards quietly, then move in." I nodded, gripping my pistol tightly. "Let's make this clean." Leo and Judie flanked the guards, their movements silent and precise. Two muffled shots later, the guards slumped to the ground. Ruby stayed close behind me as we slipped through the gate, our steps cautious. The courtyard was eerily quiet, the villa's grand façade looming over us. The guards on the balcony were patrolling lazily, their rifles slung over their shoulders.

"Mia, disable the lights," I whispered.

"On it," she replied.

The floodlights flickered once before plunging the courtyard into darkness. The guards on the balcony cursed, their voices sharp as they tried to adjust to the sudden change. Leo didn't give them the chance. Three silenced shots rang out, and the guards dropped, their bodies crumpling against the railings.

"Clear," Leo said, his voice low.

We moved toward the main entrance, Ruby at my side. I could feel her unease, but she kept pace, her eyes scanning for any sign of danger. Inside, the villa was a maze of opulent hallways and dimly lit rooms. The air was heavy with the scent of cigars and expensive cologne—a stark reminder of the world Dante inhabited. We stopped at a large set of double doors, the muffled sound of voices emanating from the other side.

"He's in there," Leo whispered.

Judie nodded, positioning herself beside the door. "On your mark." I glanced at Ruby, who gave me a small, tense nod. Despite everything, she was here, trusting me, even if just for this moment.

"Now," I said.

Leo kicked the door open, and chaos erupted. Dante and his men were gathered around a long table, their weapons drawn the moment we burst in. Bullets tore through the air, shattering glass and splintering wood. I dove behind an overturned couch, firing at anything that moved. Ruby stayed low, taking cover behind a heavy column.

Dante's voice rang out over the gunfire, mocking and cold. "You never learn, Ryan! You can't outrun your past!" I gritted my teeth, my focus narrowing as I spotted him at the far end of the room. He was flanked by two men, their guns trained on us.

"Leo, cover me!" I shouted, breaking from cover.

Leo laid down suppressing fire as I advanced, each step a battle against the pain in my side and back. Dante raised his pistol, aiming directly at me. "This is where it ends!" he snarled. I fired first. The bullet caught him in the shoulder, sending him stumbling back. His men hesitated, and that was all the opening Leo and Judie needed. Within seconds, the room fell silent, the air thick with smoke and the scent of gunpowder. Dante was on the ground, clutching his wounded shoulder. I stood over him, my pistol trained on his head.

"You think killing me will fix everything?" he spat.

"No," I said, my voice cold. "But it's a start."

Before I could pull the trigger, Ruby's voice cut through the haze.

"Ryan, stop."

I turned to see her standing a few feet away, her eyes locked on mine.

"If you do this, you're no better than him," she said, her voice steady despite the tremor in her hands.

Her words hit me like a freight train, and for a moment, the room seemed to tilt. Dante laughed weakly, his head rolling back. "Listen to her, Ryan. Maybe she's smarter than you." I tightened my grip on the pistol, every muscle in my body screaming for release. But Ruby's gaze held me in place, grounding me.

With a deep breath, I lowered the gun.

"Cuff him," I said to Leo, my voice hoarse.

As Dante was dragged away, Ruby stepped closer, her hand brushing against mine.

"You made the right choice," she said softly.

I wasn't so sure. But as I looked into her eyes, I realized that, for the first time in a long time, I wanted to believe I had. The adrenaline that had carried me through the confrontation began to wane, replaced by a gnawing exhaustion and the sharp, relentless pain of my wounds. Leo and Judie secured Dante to a chair, his snarl now silenced by a strip of duct tape across his mouth. His men lay lifeless around us, their weapons scattered across the ornate room. Ruby stood close, her eyes flicking from Dante to me, her expression unreadable. I could tell she was still processing everything—the lies, the truth, the choices we'd made.

"You're bleeding again," she said quietly, motioning to my chest.

I looked down, grimacing at the dark stain spreading across my shirt. "I've had worse." She didn't respond, but the concern in her gaze was impossible to miss. Ruby wasn't the type to let emotions cloud her judgment, but I knew she was struggling to balance her feelings with the harsh realities of the situation.

"We need to move," Leo said, breaking the silence. "Dante's crew will notice he's gone soon, and I don't want to be here when they do."

Judie nodded, already gathering intel from Dante's table. "Looks like they were planning a large-scale assault. These maps detail your estate and the surrounding areas. They've been watching you for months." I exhaled sharply, anger simmering just beneath the surface. "He's not leaving this room until he tells me everything." Dante groaned behind the tape, his eyes narrowing with hatred.

"Ryan," Ruby said, stepping in front of me. "We don't have time for this. If his men are on their way, we're sitting ducks."

She was right, but leaving Dante alive felt like a loose thread waiting to unravel. My grip tightened around the pistol in my hand. Leo placed a firm hand on my shoulder. "We've got what we need. Let's get the hell out of here before this turns into a bloodbath." Reluctantly, I nodded. "Judie, get the car ready. Leo, secure Dante in the trunk. He's coming with us." Ruby frowned. "What are you planning to do with him?"

"Get the truth," I said, my voice hard.

Her jaw tightened, but she didn't argue.

We navigated the dark forest roads in tense silence, the weight of everything hanging heavy in the air. Ruby sat beside me, her hands resting in her lap, but her posture was rigid. I wanted to reach out to her, to bridge the growing distance between us, but I didn't know where to start. In the back, Dante was barely conscious, his head lolling against the side of the trunk. Judie kept her weapon trained on him, just in case.

"We're being followed," Mia's voice came through the comms, sharp and urgent.

Leo glanced in the rearview mirror, his knuckles whitening on the steering wheel. "How many?"

"Three SUVs. They're closing fast."

Ruby's eyes snapped to me, fear and resolve warring in her expression. "What do we do?" I grabbed my rifle, ignoring the flare of pain in my chest. "We stop running." Leo veered off the road, pulling into a clearing surrounded by dense trees. The SUVs skidded to a halt behind us, men spilling out, their weapons glinting in the moonlight.

"Judie, take Ruby and get to cover," I ordered.

"I'm not leaving you," Ruby said, her voice firm.

I turned to her, my gaze steady. "Please, Ruby. Let me keep you safe." Her lips pressed into a thin line, but she nodded reluctantly, following Judie into the shadows. The first shots rang out, slicing through the silence. Leo and I took cover behind the SUV, returning fire as Dante's men advanced trying to keep them from getting to Dante. The forest erupted into chaos, muzzle flashes lighting up the darkness as bullets tore through branches and bark. I pushed through the pain, my focus narrowing to the battle before me. Dante's men were relentless, but Leo and I held our ground, forcing them to take cover. A grenade rolled into the clearing, its metal surface glinting ominously.

> "Move!" I shouted, grabbing Leo and diving for cover as the explosion ripped through the air.

The blast sent debris flying, the shockwave slamming into me like a freight train. My ears rang as I pushed myself up, my vision swimming. In the distance, I saw Ruby crouched low behind a fallen tree, her wide eyes locking onto mine.

> "We're outnumbered!" Leo shouted, firing at an advancing group.

I gritted my teeth, my grip tightening on my rifle. "We've been through worse." More gunfire erupted, the odds stacked against us. My chest burned with every breath, and I could feel the blood loss taking its toll, but I refused to back down.

"Ryan!" Ruby's voice cut through the chaos, sharp and desperate.

I turned just in time to see a figure aiming at me from the trees. I raised my rifle, but my body was slow, weakened. The shot rang out before I could react, a searing pain ripping through my chest. I staggered back, the world tilting dangerously.

"Ryan!" Ruby broke cover, sprinting toward me despite the gunfire.

Leo grabbed her arm, pulling her down as he fired at the attacker.

"Stay with me," Ruby pleaded, her hands pressing against my chest to stem the bleeding.

My vision blurred, her face swimming in and out of focus. "I'm sorry, I should have stayed at the estate, I'm not... going anywhere." I saw Ruby's tear-filled eyes and the faint silhouette of Leo standing over us, his rifle blazing. "Judie! Leo, yelled. "Get the car ready, ill cover you. We need to move now!" The ride was a blur of pain and motion. Ruby refused to let go, her hands still applying pressure to the wound in my chest. Her face was pale, her lips pressed into a thin line as she fought to keep me conscious.

"Keep talking to me," she said, her voice trembling but determined.

"I'm fine," I lied, my voice barely audible.

Her laugh was bitter. "You've been shot three times and a fourth time now in two nights, Ryan. Don't start lying to me now." I managed a weak smile, but her words hit harder than I expected. The lie about my past still hung between us, an unspoken weight that had fractured the trust we'd built. Yet here she was, fighting to keep me alive. The

SUV jolted as Judie swerved to avoid something on the road, pulling me out of my thoughts.

"We're heading to the secondary safe house," Leo said from the front seat. "We can regroup there, but we've got to patch him up fast."

Ruby's eyes met mine, her fear barely concealed. "You're going to make it, Ryan. Do you hear me?" Her words weren't a plea—they were a command. We reached the safe house just as the first light of dawn crept over the horizon. The building was unassuming, tucked away in a dense forest far from prying eyes. Leo and Judie worked quickly to secure the perimeter, leaving Ruby and me alone in the small, dimly lit living room.

"You need to lie down," she said firmly, her tone leaving no room for argument.

I let her guide me to the couch, though every step felt like fire coursing through my veins. She grabbed a first aid kit from a nearby shelf and knelt beside me, her hands steady despite the panic simmering just below the surface.

"Take off your shirt," she instructed, already reaching for the shears to cut away the blood-soaked fabric.

I gritted my teeth as the cool air hit the wounds. Ruby didn't flinch as she examined them, her focus razor-sharp.

"This is going to hurt," she warned, holding up a needle and thread.

I nodded, bracing myself. Her hands moved with precision, stitching up the gashes with a calmness that belied the storm raging in her eyes.

"You've done this before," I muttered, trying to distract myself from the pain.

Her lips twitched in the faintest ghost of a smile. "You're not the only one who's lived through chaos." We worked in silence for a while, the only sounds the crackle of the fireplace and the occasional hiss of my breath as she patched me up. When she finally finished, she sat back on her heels, wiping her hands on a towel.

"You'll live," she said, her voice soft but tired.

"Thanks to you," I replied.

Her eyes met mine, and for a moment, the tension between us eased. But then her gaze hardened. "We need to talk about what happens next." I nodded. "We will. But first, I need to know if you're okay."

"Me?" she asked, incredulous. "I'm not the one riddled with bullets, Ryan."

"No, but you've been carrying the weight of all this too," I said. "And I know I haven't made it easier."

Her expression softened, but the crack in her armour didn't last long. "We'll deal with that later. Right now, we need to focus on the people coming for us."

"They're not just coming for me," I admitted, my voice low.

"They're coming for everything I tried to leave behind."

Ruby stood, pacing the length of the room. "Then it's time you stop running from it and face whatever it is head-on. Because if we don't, they're going to keep coming." I leaned back against the couch, exhaustion pulling at me. "You're right." Her steps faltered. "I am?" I nodded. "I've been running from this for too long. It's time to take the fight to them. But I need you to trust me, Ruby. Even if I can't undo the mistakes I've made, I need you to believe in us." She stopped, her back to me. For a long moment, she didn't move. Then, slowly, she turned around.

"I want to," she said, her voice barely above a whisper. "But trust isn't just about words, Ryan. It's about actions. Prove to me that we're on the same side, and I'll follow you anywhere."

Her words hit harder than any bullet. But they were what I needed to hear.

"Then let's finish this," I said, forcing myself to sit up despite the pain. "Together."

Her eyes held mine, and for the first time in what felt like forever, I saw a flicker of hope. Leo entered the room then, his expression grim. "We've got movement on the perimeter. They've found us." Ruby's gaze snapped to me, her fear returning.

"Get ready," I said, pulling myself to my feet. "This ends now."

The safe house was a fortress, but even fortresses could fall under siege. Gunfire ricocheted off the reinforced walls, the attackers relentless in their assault. The once-quiet sanctuary was now a battlefield, and we were fighting to hold our ground. Leo stood near a window, returning fire with deadly precision. His team had fortified key entry points, using overturned furniture and steel barriers to create defensive strongholds. Judie crouched by the doorway, her weapon trained on the hall leading to the rear of the safe house. Ruby stayed low behind a heavy steel desk in the corner, her wide eyes locked on me as I moved. She didn't speak, but I could see the tension in her clenched fists, the fear she tried to hide.

"Front line is holding," Leo barked over the cacophony. "But they're regrouping. We need to end this before they breach."

I nodded, pressing a hand to my side where the earlier gunshot still burned. Blood seeped through my shirt, but I ignored it. There wasn't time to feel pain.

"Judie, Mia, hold the back," I ordered, my voice firm despite the fatigue clawing at me. "Leo and I will keep the front."

Ruby's voice cut through the chaos. "Ryan, you're already hurt. You can't—"

"I'm fine," I said, cutting her off. "Stay low. Don't move until I say."

Her eyes flashed with frustration, but she didn't argue. Instead, she pressed herself tighter against the desk, her hand hovering near the small handgun she carried.

Another explosion rocked the safe house, shaking the walls and sending dust raining from the ceiling. The front door groaned under the pressure, the attackers using everything at their disposal to force their way inside.

"They're pushing hard," Mia called from the back. "We won't hold them forever!"

"We don't need forever," I said, grabbing Leo's shoulder. "We just need long enough."

Leo grinned, his usual grim humour shining through even in the chaos. "Then let's make it count." The two of us moved to the main entryway, our weapons raised. Bullets peppered the steel-reinforced door, and I could see the hinges straining under the assault.

"On my mark," I said, raising my rifle. "Three... two..."

Before I could finish, the door burst inward, the attackers pouring through in a tide of black-clad bodies. Leo and I opened fire, cutting down the first wave before they could fully breach.

> "Fall back!" I yelled as more attackers surged forward. "Hold the second line!"

We retreated to the secondary barricade, the sound of gunfire deafening. Leo fired in controlled bursts, taking down anyone who tried to advance. I moved to cover his flank, my vision blurring from the blood loss as my wounds has opened again, but my resolve unshaken.

"Ryan, you're hit again?" Leo shouted, his voice tinged with concern.

"No, old wounds opening!" I replied, gritting my teeth. "We're not losing this."

Suddenly, the attackers' fire shifted, focusing on the rear of the house. Judie's voice crackled over the comms. "They're trying to split us! Ryan, we need—" Her words were drowned out by another explosion, this one closer. The rear wall trembled, and I knew we were running out of time.

"Ruby!" I called, turning toward her. "Stay down—"

But she wasn't where I had left her. Panic surged through me until I spotted her crawling toward the overturned barrier in the corner. She met my gaze, her expression hard with determination.

"Ruby, no—"

"I'm not leaving you!" she shouted, her voice fierce.

Before I could argue, the front line broke again, and another wave of attackers spilled into the room. Leo and I stood our ground, firing at every moving target. My body screamed in protest, my strength waning with every second, but I refused to fall. Then, just as the enemy seemed overwhelming, backup arrived. Judie's voice came over the comms, triumphant. "Reinforcements incoming! Hold your positions!" The sound of tires screeching outside was followed by a fresh wave of gunfire—this time directed at the attackers. Mia's team had arrived, their precision striking the enemy from behind and driving them into disarray. Within moments, the tide turned. The attackers scattered, their assault broken by the combined force of our defence and Mia's reinforcements. As the last of them fled into the night, silence finally fell over the safe house. My knees buckled, and I leaned heavily against the barricade, my vision swimming. Ruby was by my side in an instant, her hands on my shoulders. "Ryan," she whispered, her voice trembling. "You're bleeding so much..."

"I'm fine," I murmured, though the words felt hollow.

"No, you're not," she said, tears brimming in her eyes. "You've been shot, Ryan. So many times."

I reached up, brushing a hand against her cheek. "It's over, Ruby. We're safe." Her expression hardened, and she shook her head. "Not until you're out of danger." Leo approached, his rifle slung over his shoulder. "We've got to move. This place isn't secure anymore." I nodded weakly, letting Ruby help me to my feet. Despite the pain, I felt a surge of relief. We had survived—barely. But the fight was far from over.

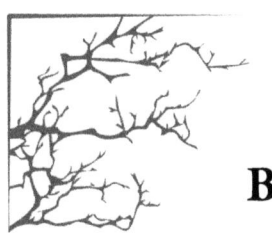

Blood and Bond

The safe house was still standing, but it felt more like a graveyard than a sanctuary. The remnants of the battle lay scattered across the floor spent shell casings, bloodstained carpets, and the bitter scent of gunpowder lingering in the air. Ruby sat beside me, her face etched with concern as I rested against the wall. Despite the adrenaline that had kept me on my feet earlier, the pain was now overwhelming. The shots to my side, back, and chest throbbed relentlessly, but I refused to show it. Not in front of her. Leo paced near the window, his eyes scanning the shadows outside, the faintest hint of worry in his expression. Even he knew this wasn't over. The enemy was out there, regrouping, likely planning their next move. Ruby didn't speak. She simply watched me, her gaze unwavering. The silence between us was thick, heavier than it had ever been before. I could feel the weight of her unspoken questions pressing on me, threatening to break the fragile barrier I had tried to build between us. She was right to be wary.

> "Ryan," Ruby finally said, her voice a soft tremor, "we need to talk about what happened. About your family. About who's really behind this."

I met her eyes. The rawness of her emotion, her frustration, and her worry, cut deeper than any bullet could. I had kept so many secrets from her, and now it seemed those secrets were unravelling, piece by painful piece.

"I told you everything," I said, my voice rough, as I reached for my water bottle. "About what I had to do to get us out of the life."

Her eyes hardened. "Did you, Ryan? Did you tell me everything?" The question hit me like a slap. I opened my mouth, but no words came out. How could I explain the depths of my family's criminal empire? The choices I had made, the deals I had struck, and the men I had betrayed... all in the name of survival. It wasn't just blood that ran through my veins. It was betrayal, lies, and the weight of a legacy I had never asked for. Ruby's breath hitched as she pushed forward, her voice low and determined. "I'm not asking you to justify it. I just need to understand. Who are we really fighting? What are we up against?" The silence stretched between us, thick and suffocating. It felt like I had already told her everything I could, but in truth, I hadn't. There was more. So much more. And the more I told her, the more I risked losing her forever. But I couldn't lie anymore.

I exhaled, my voice hoarse. "My family wasn't just some group of petty criminals, Ruby. We ran an empire. My father—he wasn't just the head of a cartel, he was one of the most dangerous men in Italy. And I was supposed to take his place." Ruby's eyes widened, the shock evident on her face. "What? Ryan, I... I didn't know." I swallowed hard, the weight of the truth crushing me. "You didn't know because I did everything I could to bury that part of me. To bury my family's legacy. But I couldn't outrun it. I tried to cut ties, but they never let me go. And now... now they're coming for us again." The room was quiet except for the sound of my ragged breathing and the soft hum of the security system. Ruby's gaze softened, her fingers brushing against mine, the touch gentle but laden with the understanding that had been missing for so long.

"Ryan, I'm with you," she said, her voice unwavering. "I'm in this with you. But I need to know what's coming. I need to know what you're up against. If I'm going to be by your side through this, we need to face it together."

Her words should have comforted me, but they only served to remind me of the depth of the darkness that was about to consume us both. She had no idea what she was stepping into. No idea what sacrifices were going to be demanded of her. I leaned back against the wall, my body screaming in protest, and looked up at her. "They're not just after me, Ruby. They're after everything I've built. Everything you and I have worked for. This isn't just about my past anymore. It's about our future." Ruby's eyes narrowed, her expression hardening. "Then let's fight for it. We'll fight for what's ours." I nodded slowly, the weight of the decision pressing down on me. "I need you to trust me," I said, my voice barely above a whisper. "This is going to get worse before it gets better. And I'm going to need you to fight just as hard as I will." She didn't hesitate. "I'm not afraid of the fight, Ryan. You know that." I took a deep breath, the sound of footsteps echoing in the hallway signalling Leo's return. The battle wasn't over, but it had changed. We were no longer just surviving. We were fighting for something bigger. Something worth fighting for.

As Leo stepped into the room, his face grim, he glanced at the two of us. "We've got movement. The attack's not over. We need to get out of here, now." Ruby stood without a word, her eyes locked on me, steady and sure. Whatever we faced next, whatever was coming, we would face it together. I stood, my legs shaky from blood loss and exhaustion, and together we moved toward the door. The storm was far from over. But now, at least, Ruby understood what we were fighting for. She understood the cost of the battle ahead. And I knew that no matter what happened, I wouldn't be facing it alone. The hallway was dimly lit, the emergency lights casting an eerie red glow over the cracked walls. I leaned heavily on Ruby as we moved, every step a battle against the burning pain in my chest and side. My breaths came in shallow gasps, each one a reminder of how close I had come to losing everything. Leo and his team formed a protective barrier around us, their movements sharp and calculated. The echoes of gunfire from earlier seemed to reverberate in the silence, a haunting reminder of the battle we had barely survived. Outside, the night was still, but we all knew it wouldn't last. We reached the safe house's central room—a makeshift command centre with screens displaying live feeds from the perimeter cameras. Mia stood by the monitors, her fingers flying over the keyboard as she adjusted the security protocols.

"We've got more incoming," she said without looking up. "Three vehicles, heavily armed. Whoever they are, they're not here to talk."

Leo muttered a curse under his breath. "We need to move. This place won't hold if they hit us again." The emergency lights in the safe house flickered as Leo and Mia gathered the explosives, their movements sharp and efficient. The tension in the air was palpable, every second ticking down toward the inevitable. I stood by the monitors, gripping the edge of the desk to stay upright, my body screaming for rest. Ruby knelt beside me, her hands deftly cleaning the blood from the wounds on my side and back.

"You're a mess," she muttered, her voice tight with frustration.

I winced as the alcohol stung. "You should see the other guy." Her laugh was bitter. "You've been shot three times and a fourth now in two nights, Ryan. Don't start lying to me now."

I glanced down at her, catching the flicker of fear and anger in her eyes, and I hated myself for putting her through this. But before I could say anything, Mia's voice crackled over the comms.

"Ryan, we're in position. Traps are set along the east and south entrances. Leo's securing the north side now."

"Good," I said, keeping my tone steady. "Make sure the blast radius covers the choke points. If they get through, we won't have the firepower to hold them off for long."

Mia's reply was clipped. "Understood." Ruby didn't stop working as she cleaned the wound on my back, though her hands trembled slightly. "Why do you do this, Ryan? Why keep putting yourself in harm's way?" I exhaled slowly, the weight of her question pressing down on me. "Because if I don't, the people I care about get hurt. I can't let that happen, Ruby. Not again." Her silence was louder than any response she could have given, but she didn't push further. Instead, she bandaged my side with a focus that bordered on angry determination. The monitors showed the advancing vehicles, their headlights piercing the darkness. I toggled the comms. "Leo, they're almost at the perimeter. Are you ready?"

"Ready as we'll ever be," came his reply.

The first explosion lit up the night like a sunrise, shaking the ground beneath us. Ruby flinched but didn't let go of me.

"That's one," Leo said over the comms. "Second vehicle's trying to push through."

The second blast followed moments later, flipping the SUV onto its side. The attackers spilled out, disoriented but still armed.

"Mia, you've got a group moving in from the south entrance," I said, my eyes glued to the screens.

"On it," she replied.

Ruby finished wrapping my wounds and stood, her gaze fierce. "What now?"

"Now," I said, straightening despite the agony in my chest, "we fight."

The attackers regrouped, their remaining numbers splitting between the north and south sides. The gunfire outside was deafening, flashes of light illuminating the dark landscape. Leo's voice crackled through the comms again.

"They're pushing hard on the north. We need backup!"

"Mia," I said, "redirect fire from the south. Keep them off Leo's position."

"Copy that," Mia answered.

Ruby stayed by my side, watching the monitors intently. Her hand brushed mine, a brief but grounding gesture. Despite everything, she was still here. Still fighting with me, even when she had every reason to walk away. The minutes stretched into what felt like hours, every second a test of our endurance. When the final explosion rocked the safe house, the remaining attackers scattered, their retreat hasty and disorganized. Leo's voice came through the comms, breathless but triumphant. "They're falling back." I leaned heavily on the desk, exhaustion threatening to pull me under. Ruby's hand was on my arm, steadying me.

"We did it," she said softly, her voice tinged with relief.

"For now," I replied, my gaze still on the monitors.

The attackers might have retreated, but this was far from over. Leo and Mia returned moments later, their faces grim but determined.

"This safe house is blown," Leo said. "They know where we are now. We need to move."

I nodded, my mind already racing with the next steps. "We'll regroup. Plan our next move. But for tonight... we survived." Ruby's hand tightened on mine, and for the first time in what felt like forever, I allowed myself to believe that we could get through this—together.

The adrenaline rush of the battle outside began to ebb, leaving an eerie stillness in its wake. The faint crackle of flames from the burning wreckage outside seeped through the walls. Leo leaned against the doorframe, his rifle slung over his shoulder. His shirt was streaked with dirt and sweat, and his expression was grim.

"They'll be back," he said, breaking the silence. "They didn't expect us to hit this hard, but next time. They'll come stronger."

I nodded, pressing a hand to my side where Ruby had bandaged me. The pain was a dull roar now, manageable but constant. "We'll be ready." Mia stepped into the room, her face illuminated by the glow of her tablet. "We've got to assume they're regrouping. I intercepted a few of their comms; they're calling for reinforcements." Ruby, still standing close to me, asked, "How much time do we have?"

"Not enough," Mia replied, her voice clipped. "We need to leave before sunrise."

Leo looked at me, his jaw tight. "We can't keep running forever, Ryan. At some point, we've got to take the fight to them."

He was right, but the thought of leading another battle with Ruby at my side made my stomach churn. I glanced at her, and the determination in her eyes told me she wasn't going to let fear hold her back.

"Not here," I said finally. "Not when we're compromised. We'll move to the secondary safe house and regroup there. We'll hit them when we're stronger."

Mia nodded, already pulling up maps and coordinates on her screen. "I'll get the vehicles ready. We'll take the southern route; it's less likely to be monitored." As Mia and Leo left the room, Ruby turned to me. Her expression was unreadable, her lips pressed into a tight line.

"You're pushing yourself too hard," she said quietly. "You're not invincible, Ryan."

"I know," I said, meeting her gaze. "But if I stop, even for a second, everything we've built die with us and I am not prepared to let that happen, I made a promise to you. To protect you and to show you I can be trusted."

Her hand found mine, her touch grounding me in the chaos. "You don't have to do it alone." I tightened my grip on her hand, the weight of the moment settling between us. "I know," I said again, softer this time. "I just need you to trust me." Ruby didn't reply immediately. Her silence spoke volumes, the conflict in her eyes tearing at me. "I want to, Ryan," she admitted, her voice barely above a whisper. "But after everything... it's hard."

"I'll prove it to you," I promised, the words raw and honest. "Whatever it takes."

Before she could respond, Leo's voice cut through the comms. "We've got movement. Looks like a scouting party heading toward the perimeter."

"Time to go," I said, forcing myself to my feet despite the sharp protest of my wounds. Ruby helped steady me, her touch lingering.

The escape was swift and tense, every shadow feeling like it could spring to life with danger. The convoy wound through back roads and dense forest, the safe house receding behind us. Ruby stayed close, her eyes scanning the dark terrain as if it could offer answers to questions neither of us could voice. When we finally reached the secondary safe house—a smaller, more secluded location tucked into the mountains—everyone moved quickly to secure the area. Leo and Mia set up surveillance, while Ruby and I retreated to a small room that smelled of pine and damp stone. As I sat on the edge of the bed, Ruby knelt before me again, carefully unwrapping the makeshift bandages. Her touch was gentle but efficient, the silence between us heavy.

"You keep putting yourself in the line of fire," she said after a moment, not looking at me. "Do you even care what happens to you?"

I caught her hand, forcing her to meet my gaze. "Of course I care. I care because if something happens to me, it happens to you too. To all of us." Her eyes glistened, but she didn't let the tears fall. "Then stop pretending you're indestructible, Ryan. Because one day, you won't get back up." The words hit me harder than any bullet ever had.

"I'll try," I said, and it was the most honest thing I could offer her in that moment.

Ruby pressed her forehead to mine, her breath mingling with mine as she whispered, "Just don't leave me. Not like this."

"I won't," I promised, the vow sealing itself in my heart. "Not ever."

As the night stretched on, the bond between us felt stronger than the blood we'd shed. Whatever came next, we'd face it together—even if the shadows of my past threatened to tear us apart. The safe house's dimly lit conference room had taken on the tense air of a battlefield negotiation. Ruby sat across from Giovanni Mancini, her posture straight, her tone calm but firm. Judie was at her side, the flicker of her calculating eyes betraying her role in this delicate operation. Mancini leaned back in his chair, his arms crossed over his chest. The bruises from his earlier scuffle with Leo had faded, but his pride had not recovered. The man's demeanour was wary, like a predator uncertain whether to strike or retreat.

"You want my people," Mancini said, his voice carrying both incredulity and suspicion. "And in exchange, you promise to keep me breathing while I'm locked in your cage?"

Ruby didn't flinch, her gaze unwavering. "That's the gist of it. You know what's out there, Giovanni. Alessandro Vitale and Francesca D'Alessandro's men won't stop at us. You're just as expendable to them as we are. With us, you'll live to see another day."

"And Dante?" Mancini's lip curled at the name, disdain evident.

Judie interjected smoothly, her voice a velvet blade. "Dante's not your problem anymore. We'll keep him in check, just like we've kept you alive. But you must give us something in return."

Mancini studied them both, his eyes narrowing. "And what makes you think my men will follow your orders? They're loyal to me, not to you." Ruby leaned forward slightly, her voice dropping to a dangerous calm. "Because they'll follow *your* orders. You'll tell them this is the only way to keep you alive. And if that's not incentive enough, remind them that working with us means taking down the people who betrayed you." The room fell into silence, the weight of her words sinking in. Mancini tapped his fingers on the table, considering.

"You're asking for a lot," he said finally. "But you're right. They won't stop until we're all dead. Fine. I'll give you, my men. But I want something in writing—proof that this protection doesn't disappear the moment I'm no longer useful to you."

Ruby nodded. "Done. Judie?"

Judie slid a pre-drafted agreement across the table, her smile cool. "Already prepared. Sign it, and we'll start coordinating with your men immediately." Mancini glanced at the paper, then at Ruby and Judie. "You two are tougher than you look. I'll give you that." Ruby didn't respond to the backhanded compliment. Instead, she placed a pen on the table and watched as Mancini signed.

The Cells

After the negotiation, Ruby and Judie descended into the holding area where Mancini and Dante were kept in separate rooms. The tension in the narrow hallway was palpable. Mancini's men had already been contacted, and the first of them were in route to bolster their defences. Now, it was time to make sure the prisoners stayed in line.

"Dante's been quiet," Mia reported as they passed her station near the surveillance monitors. "Too quiet. You sure we shouldn't just get rid of him?"

Ruby's expression was unreadable. "We might still need him." She stopped outside Mancini's cell, nodding for the guard to let her in. Mancini was seated on the cot, his hands resting on his knees.

"Your men are mobilizing," Ruby informed him. "This works for both of us. Don't forget that."

"I haven't," Mancini replied, his voice low. "But you'd better be sure you can trust me, Mrs. Giovannetti. Because if you can't..."

Ruby interrupted, her tone icy. "I know exactly who you are, Giovanni. And I know what you're capable of. But understand this—we're not doing this because we trust you. We're doing this because we're out of options. Betray us, and you'll wish you stayed with

Dante." Mancini's smile didn't reach his eyes, but he nodded. "Fair enough."

In the War Room

Back upstairs, Ruby rejoined Ryan, who was monitoring the incoming feeds. His complexion was pale, and every movement betrayed the pain he was still enduring, but his eyes were sharp.

"How'd it go?" he asked without looking up.

"Signed and sealed," Ruby replied. "Mancini's men are ours, at least for now."

Ryan glanced at her, something akin to pride flickering in his gaze. "Good work." She didn't respond immediately, instead moving to stand beside him. "How are you holding up?"

"Not bad for someone who's been shot four times in two nights," he said, attempting a wry smile.

Her lips curved faintly, but her concern was evident. "We're buying time, Ryan. But that's all it is—time. Sooner or later, Alessandro Vitale and Francesca D'Alessandro's men is going to hit us with everything they've got." Ryan leaned back in his chair, his jaw tightening. "Then we'd better make sure we're ready." Ruby's hand brushed his shoulder, a quiet reminder that, for all the fractures between them, they were still in this together.

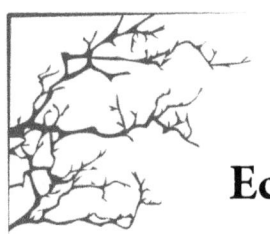

Echoes of Betrayal

The walls of the safe house felt smaller now, as if the weight of everything pressing down on us had seeped into the very structure. Outside, the gunfire had dulled to sporadic bursts, the traps and Mancini's reinforcements doing their part to keep Vitale's men at bay—for now. Inside, it was far quieter, but the silence carried its own tension. Ruby sat across from me, arms crossed tightly over her chest, her eyes fixed on the floor. She'd been like that since the negotiation ended, and I knew better than to push her. But the longer the silence stretched, the heavier it became.

"You made the right call," I said, breaking it.

Her head snapped up, her gaze sharp. "Did I?" I leaned back, wincing as the movement pulled at the bandages on my chest and back. "If Mancini's men hadn't come through, we wouldn't be having this conversation right now."

> "That's not what I mean," she shot back. "I had to promise protection to a man who has as much blood on his hands as you do. And why? Because your past keeps crawling out of the shadows to kill us."

Her words cut deeper than the bullets I'd taken, but I couldn't deny the truth in them.

"Ruby—"

> "No." She stood, pacing the small room. "You've been shot four times in two nights, Ryan. Four. And I've been right

here, patching you up, watching you bleed, and I can't even—" She broke off, exhaling sharply. "I don't know if I can keep doing this."

I wanted to reach for her, but something in her posture held me back. Instead, I forced myself to stay seated, to let her speak.

"You keep telling me you didn't want to involve me in your past," she said, her voice quieter now but no less sharp. "But it's not just your past, Ryan. It's your present. It's your future. It's... it's us."

"Ruby," I said, standing slowly. "I never wanted this for you. For us. But I can't change who I was, and I can't undo the things I've done."

She turned to face me, and for a moment, I saw something flicker in her eyes—fear, anger, maybe even love. "Then what happens when this is over?" I didn't have an answer.

Cracks in the Armor

The tension between us hung heavy as I returned to the monitors. Leo's voice came through the comms.

"Ryan, you there?"

"Yeah," I said, clearing my throat. "Status?"

"We're holding, but just barely. Vitale's sending another wave. They're getting bolder, like they know we're running out of options."

I glanced at Ruby, who had stopped pacing and was now leaning against the wall, her arms still crossed.

"We'll need to fall back," I said into the comms. "Consolidate inside the safe house. Keep them funnelled into our kill zones."

"Got it," Leo replied. "But Ryan... something doesn't sit right. They're too organized. This isn't just Vitale and D'Alessandro taking a shot in the dark. Someone's feeding them intel." I stiffened, the implications hitting me like a gut punch. "You think we've got a mole?"

"Has to be," Leo said. "They know our traps, our defences. Hell, they knew about this safe house."

Ruby's head snapped up at that, her eyes locking onto mine.

"Stay sharp," I said, my voice tight. "We'll regroup once this wave is down."

As the comm went quiet, Ruby stepped forward. "A mole?"
"Looks like it," I said.
"And you think it's someone inside?"
I didn't answer right away. The truth was, I didn't want to believe it. But Leo was right—Vitale and D'Alessandro had been too precise in their attacks. Someone was giving them information. Ruby's jaw tightened. "Do you think it's Mancini?"

"Unlikely," I said. "He wouldn't have sent his men to help us if he was working with them."

"Then who?"
The question hung in the air, unspoken accusations hovering between us.

Breaking Point

An explosion rocked the safe house, shaking the walls and sending dust raining down from the ceiling. The comm crackled again, Leo's voice urgent.

"They're breaching the north side! We need reinforcements now!"

As the gunfire intensified, I couldn't shake the feeling that this was just the beginning. The mole, the betrayal, the cracks in our bond—they were all pieces of a puzzle I didn't yet understand. But one thing was certain: the echoes of my past were growing louder, and they wouldn't stop until they consumed us. As the chaos of the attack wore on, every second felt heavier, the weight of betrayal sinking deeper into my chest than any bullet ever could. Ruby was back at the monitors, her hands hovering over the controls while keeping an eye on the comms. Leo and Mia were holding the north breach, but Vitale's men were relentless, forcing us into tighter defences. Julie stood in the corner, pacing as her phone pressed against her ear. Her face was set in a mask of determination, her tone low and urgent.

"Luca," she said, her voice cutting through the tension like steel. "It's time. I need you and your people now."

Luca. The name hit me like a cold gust of wind. I remembered him vividly—the man who had revealed Julie's survival to me and Ruby years ago. He was a phantom, a shadow that lingered behind her, fiercely loyal and terrifyingly efficient.

"I know," Julie continued, her voice softening slightly. "I wouldn't have called if it wasn't life or death. It's Ryan and Ruby. They need u."

There was a pause, her expression unchanging as she listened. Finally, she nodded. "Thank you. Be quick." She hung up and turned to face me.

"Luca?" I asked, trying to ignore the pang of uncertainty the name stirred.

"You don't survive in my world without someone like him," Julie said matter-of-factly. "He's been my right hand for years—long before you even knew I was alive. And now, he's bringing his people to help us."

I glanced at Ruby, who was still monitoring the fight on the screens. Her face was pale, but she didn't react to Julie's words. Not outwardly, at least.

"Julie," I said, my voice low. "If this goes south..."

"It won't," she interrupted. "Luca is loyal to me, and his men are a force to be reckoned with. They'll turn the tide."

I nodded, not entirely reassured but knowing we didn't have any better options.

Reinforcements

It wasn't long before the roar of engines filled the air outside the safe house. The monitors lit up with the sight of a convoy of black SUVs speeding toward the fight. The men who emerged were unlike anything Vitale's forces had brought to bear—disciplined, heavily armed, and moving with lethal precision.

At their head was Luca. His presence was commanding, his sharp features and cold eyes betraying nothing as he directed his men.

"Luca," Julie greeted him as he entered the safe house.

He gave her a small nod, his gaze flickering to me. "Ryan. It's been a while."

"Not long enough," I said, though my tone lacked venom.

He smirked faintly, then turned to Julie. "What's the plan?" Julie quickly briefed him on the situation, and he relayed orders to his men with practiced efficiency. Within minutes, the tide of the battle began to shift. Vitale's forces were being pushed back, their numbers dwindling under the combined assault of Leo's team and Luca's reinforcements.

The Aftermath

As the last echoes of gunfire faded, Ruby sank into a chair, her shoulders slumping in exhaustion. I leaned against the wall, my bandaged wounds burning with every breath, but I forced myself to stay upright. Julie approached, her expression unreadable. "We've bought some time," she said. "But they'll be back. Vitale and Francesca won't stop until we're gone." I nodded, my thoughts spinning. "Then we make the next move." Ruby looked up at me, her eyes wary but resolute. "What's the plan?"

> "We take the fight to them," I said. "No more waiting. No more reacting. It's time to end this."

The room fell silent, the weight of my words settling over everyone. Luca broke the silence, his voice steady. "If that's the plan, we'll follow. But you'd better make it count, Ryan."

I met his gaze, my jaw tightening. "Oh, I intend to." Ruby stood, her eyes meeting mine. There was still a flicker of doubt in her expression, but there was something else, too—determination.

"Then let's do it," she said, her voice firm.

Julie nodded, a faint smile playing on her lips. "It's about time we stopped running." The decision to strike first was made swiftly. Vitale and Francesca had underestimated us for the last time, and we weren't going to waste the momentum Luca's arrival had given us. Our combined forces—my men, Leo and Mia's team, Luca's formidable operatives, and what remained of Mancini's loyalists—formed a powerful coalition. It wasn't just about survival anymore; it was about taking back control.

Preparing for the Fight

The safe house buzzed with coordinated activity as plans were laid out. Maps were spread across tables, and every angle of attack was scrutinized. Vitale and Francesca had holed up in an abandoned villa on the outskirts of the city, turning it into their operational hub. It was heavily fortified, but not impregnable. Luca stood at the centre of it all, his calm presence commanding respect. "We'll hit them from two sides," he said, his voice even. "My men will create a distraction at the west entrance while you and your team breach from the east." Leo nodded. "Once we're inside, it's about speed. We can't let them regroup."

"Agreed," I said, glancing at Ruby, who stood nearby, arms crossed. She hadn't spoken much, but her presence was steady, grounding. "Ruby, you'll stay with Julie and oversee the comms. We'll need eyes everywhere."

She opened her mouth to argue but stopped, her lips pressing into a thin line. "Fine," she said finally. "But if things go south, I'm coming in." I gave her a small nod, knowing better than to argue further.

The Assault

The night was dark, the moon hidden behind thick clouds as our convoy approached the villa. The tension in the air was palpable, the weight of what we were about to do pressing heavily on all of us. From my position in the lead SUV, I watched as Luca's men silently moved into position. They were ghosts in the shadows, their movements precise and unyielding. The first explosion came from the west, a fiery eruption that lit up the sky and sent Vitale's guards scrambling. The diversion worked perfectly, pulling their attention away from our approach.

"Move," I said over the comms, and we surged forward.

Breaching the Villa

The east entrance was lightly guarded, and we took down the sentries with swift efficiency. Inside, the villa was a maze of corridors and rooms, but we moved with purpose, clearing each space methodically. Gunfire erupted as Vitale's men engaged us, the sharp cracks of bullets echoing off the walls. I stayed close to Leo and Mia, my movements slower than usual thanks to my injuries but no less determined. Luca's voice came through the comms. "West team is inside. We're pinning down their reinforcements."

"Good," I replied, ducking behind cover as a hail of bullets shattered a nearby vase. "Keep them there."

Confrontation

As we pushed deeper into the villa, it became clear that Vitale and Francesca were prepared for a siege. Their men fought fiercely, using the layout of the villa to their advantage. But our combined forces were relentless, and their defences began to crumble. Finally, we reached the heart of the villa—a grand hall where Vitale and Francesca had made their stand. They were surrounded by their most loyal guards, the air thick with tension.

"Ryan Giovannetti," Vitale called out, his voice dripping with disdain. "You've brought quite the entourage. Are you here to beg for mercy?"

I stepped forward, my gun trained on him. "No. I'm here to end this." Francesca sneered, her pistol aimed at me. "Bold words for a man who's bleeding out."

"You should've stayed out of our way," I said, my voice cold.

The room exploded into chaos as the first shots were fired.

The Final Push

The battle was fierce, every shot fired carrying the weight of betrayal and vengeance. Vitale's men were skilled, but they were outnumbered and outmanoeuvred. Luca's operatives were a force of nature, their precision and ruthlessness unmatched. Leo and Mia moved like a well-oiled machine, covering each other as they picked off guards one by one. I pushed forward, my focus singular: Vitale and Francesca.

Vitale was the first to fall, a well-placed shot from Luca taking him down. Francesca, however, was not so easily subdued. She fought with the desperation of a cornered animal, her eyes wild as she fired wildly into the fray. It was Ruby's voice over the comms that guided us to her. "Ryan, she's heading for the south wing. Cut her off!" I nodded to Leo, and together we pursued her. The chase ended in a small library, where she made her final stand.

"It's over, Francesca," I said, my gun trained on her.

She laughed, the sound hollow. "You think this ends with me? You'll never escape this life, Giovannetti. It's in your blood." Her words hung in the air, but they didn't stop me from pulling the trigger...

Aftermath

The villa was silent now, the smoke from the battle still lingering in the air. Vitale and Francesca were gone, their reign of terror ended. Ruby and Julie joined us in the hall, their expressions a mix of relief and exhaustion.

"It's done," I said, my voice heavy.

Ruby looked at me, her eyes softening. "For now." Julie placed a hand on my shoulder. "You did what needed to be done. But you know this isn't over." I nodded, the weight of her words sinking in. We had won the battle, but the war was far from over.

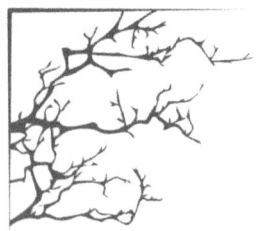

The Silent War

The aftermath of the villa battle left us with fleeting relief but no real peace. Victory had come at a cost, and the scars—physical and emotional—were already settling in. As the hours stretched into days, the war transformed, no longer fought in explosive clashes but in calculated moves and subtle strikes. Our enemies had gone quiet, but that silence was more dangerous than gunfire.

The Gathering Storm

We regrouped back at the estate, which had been fortified to the brink. The safe house was still too exposed, and with Vitale and Francesca eliminated, the focus shifted to uncovering the true extent of their allies and influence. Ruby sat across from me in the library, her arms folded, her face unreadable. Between us was a map marked with names and locations—people who'd worked with Vitale and Francesca, remnants of their fractured network.

> "We need to anticipate their next move," she said finally, her voice steady. "If we react, we're always behind. We must make them show their hand."
>
> "And how do we do that?" Leo asked, leaning against the doorframe. "They've gone underground. No chatter, no moves, no nothing."

Ruby's gaze didn't waver. "We make them think we're weaker than we are. That we're vulnerable." Leo frowned, but I caught the thread of her plan. "You're talking about bait," I said. She nodded. "We must force them to come to us. And when they do, we'll be ready."

Laying the Trap

It didn't take long to set things in motion. Julie and Luca coordinated the larger strategy, deploying their forces strategically to create the illusion of gaps in our defences. Mia worked tirelessly on the tech side, planting false leads and leaking information that painted us as fractured and scrambling. Ruby, however, had the most dangerous role.

> "I'll negotiate," she said, standing firm in the face of my protest. "You need someone they won't see as a direct threat. Someone they'll talk to."

> "You're not putting yourself in their crosshairs," I snapped, my frustration boiling over.

> "I'm already in their crosshairs," she shot back. "We all are. But I can get into their heads, Ryan. I can make them doubt themselves, doubt each other. Let me do this."

Julie stepped in before the argument escalated further. "Ruby's right. She has a talent for reading people. But she won't go alone." I clenched my fists, hating the risk but knowing it was the right move. "Fine. But if anything feels off, we pull the plug. No questions asked." Ruby nodded, her expression softening slightly. "I trust you, Ryan. Trust me too."

The Negotiation

The meeting was arranged in a neutral location—a dimly lit warehouse on the outskirts of town. Ruby and Julie went in together, their calm exteriors masking the tension simmering beneath the surface. Luca, Leo, and I waited nearby with a strike team, ready to intervene at the first sign of trouble. Inside, the air was thick with unease. Two men representing one of Vitale's remaining allies sat at a metal table, their expressions guarded.

"Ruby Giovannetti," one of them said, his voice laced with suspicion. "You've got guts coming here after what your husband did."

Ruby didn't flinch. "And yet, here you are, agreeing to meet. That says a lot about how much you're losing without Vitale and Francesca." Julie leaned forward, her presence as commanding as ever. "We're offering you a chance to step out of the chaos alive. Work with us, and you'll have protection. Refuse, and you'll find yourselves next on the list." The men exchanged glances, their resolve wavering. Ruby's calm, perceptive gaze pinned them in place.

"You don't have to like us," she said. "But you need us. And you know it."

The silence stretched, tension building, until finally, one of the men sighed. "We'll consider your terms." It wasn't a victory, but it was enough.

The Silent Attack

The trap was sprung not long after. The information Ruby and Julie fed to Vitale's remnants worked better than expected, drawing their forces out into the open. Luca's men struck first, dismantling a convoy meant to reinforce one of their strongholds. Leo and Mia's team followed suit, taking down a critical supply route. From the estate, I coordinated the operation, my wounds still fresh but my focus razor-sharp. Ruby stayed by my side, her intuition and quick thinking proving invaluable as we anticipated and countered every move.

"We're turning the tide," she said quietly, her hand brushing mine as she leaned over the monitors.

"For now," I replied, meeting her gaze. "But we can't stop until it's over."

She nodded, her determination matching my own.

The Cost of Silence

By the time the night ended, we had crippled another piece of the enemy network. But the victory was bittersweet. Every step forward brought us closer to the heart of the war, where the stakes were higher, and the cost even greater. Ruby sat beside me in the quiet aftermath, her head resting on my shoulder. "We'll get through this," she murmured, more to herself than to me. I placed a hand over hers, squeezing gently. "Together."

The war wasn't over, but in that moment, we found a sliver of peace. The tension in the estate was palpable. With each passing day, the silence from our enemies only grew heavier, a stifling pressure that gnawed at my nerves. But beneath the quiet, I knew they were regrouping. Planning. Waiting for the perfect moment to strike again. They hadn't disappeared. They were just biding their time.

And so were we.

Preparing for the Unknown

Ruby and I spent the next few days moving through the estate with precision. Every room was fortified, every entry point covered. Mia monitored the security feeds, alerting us to any potential weaknesses in our defences, while Julie and Luca worked to shore up our external operations. But it was Ruby who had become the anchor for all of us. I'd never fully understood her ability to read people, to decipher what was unsaid in a room full of noise. But now, it felt like a superpower. Every conversation we had, every strategy session, she would listen to every word and carefully sift through what wasn't being said, what was being concealed beneath the surface. It was like a game of chess, and Ruby had the sharpest mind at the table.

"I think it's time we take the offensive," Ruby said as we sat together in the war room, surrounded by monitors and maps of the city. "We know they're lying low, but we also know they won't stay that way forever. It's time to provoke them."

I frowned, my fingers tapping on the table. "We've been provoking them for weeks now, Ruby. But they're smart. They won't take the bait unless it's exactly right."

"You're right. But we've got something they don't expect. Us. And they're running out of places to hide." She stood, her eyes narrowing in focus. "I know what needs to be done. And I'm ready to go further than they think I will."

The weight of her words hit me hard. She had always been the steady one, the rational one. But this? It sounded like she was willing to cross a line.

"Ruby..." I began, but she cut me off.

"Don't argue with me, Ryan," she said, her voice firm. "We've fought this battle on their terms long enough. It's time we made them fight ours."

I could see it in her eyes: she wasn't asking for permission. She was telling me this was the way forward.

"I'm not worried about the danger," I replied, standing up and moving closer to her. "I'm worried about losing you."

She met my gaze, her hand finding mine, her grip tight. "You won't lose me. Not this time. We're in this together. But I'm not sitting back while they tear apart everything we've built."

The First Strike

Ruby and Julie worked in tandem, crafting a plan that would draw our enemies into the open. By leaking false intelligence, we hoped to lure them into attacking a critical supply chain we'd set up as bait. The idea was simple: make them think they had the upper hand. Let them feel secure, like they were getting exactly what they wanted. Then, we'd strike.

Mia kept the communication lines open, monitoring every movement, while Luca and his men prepared to move in when the trap was triggered. I stayed close to the monitors, guiding the teams through the next phase, while Ruby worked beside me, organizing everything down to the smallest detail. For hours, we waited, the silence in the air almost unbearable. My injuries from the previous night's still ached, but the adrenaline pumping through my veins kept me sharp. My mind wasn't on the pain. It was on the fight ahead. Finally, the signal came through. A message from Leo: the enemy had taken the bait. Ruby's eyes met mine, her expression a mixture of determination and something more—an understanding that this battle was unlike any we'd fought before.

"This is it," she whispered.

I nodded, giving her a brief smile. "Let's end this."

The Battle Unfolds

The ensuing firefight was brutal. We had set up a defensive perimeter around the supposed target—an abandoned factory on the outskirts of the city. Luca's men moved in first, planting explosives in strategic locations. Mia monitored the enemy's movements, feeding us vital intel. Ruby and I were stationed near the front line, watching as the enemy approached, unaware that they were walking into a trap. The gunfire erupted suddenly, echoing through the night as the enemy took the bait and began their assault. Luca's men were the first to retaliate, sending a volley of fire back at the attackers. Ruby was by my side, her eyes never leaving the field, guiding me with her sharp instincts as we exchanged fire. We took cover behind a stack of crates, the sound of bullets slicing through the air deafening.

"They're breaking through," she said, voice steady despite the chaos. "We need to push them back, now."

I nodded. "Cover me." I moved to a more exposed position, firing at anything that moved. Every muscle in my body screamed with the strain, but I didn't let up. Not now. Not when we were this close to the end. Ruby's voice came through the comms, her tone urgent but calm. "We've got reinforcements inbound, but we need to hold them off for a few more minutes. They're regrouping." I exchanged fire with one of the enemy's soldiers, taking him down with a precise shot. But just as I shifted positions, a bullet whizzed past my shoulder. I didn't flinch. The fight was far from over. Then, from the shadows, Leo and his team emerged, taking the enemy by surprise. The balance shifted. We had the advantage now.

Turning the Tide

With the reinforcements from Luca's men and Leo's team, the enemy's forces began to dwindle. The tide of battle had turned in our favour, but we couldn't afford to lose focus. Ruby was at my side the whole time, moving with the ease of someone who had fought this battle before, not once showing fear, not once faltering. But even as we took down wave after wave of enemy soldiers, I couldn't shake the feeling that something was wrong. That this wasn't the end. As the last of the enemy forces retreated into the night, I met Ruby's gaze, her face streaked with dirt and sweat. But there was a fire in her eyes that I hadn't seen before. She was ready for whatever came next. And so was I. The sound of gunfire had finally died down, but the lingering tension was far from over. The battle outside had been intense—our enemies driven back, but not defeated. The night air, thick with smoke and the smell of gunpowder, hung heavily around the estate. Inside, the atmosphere was just as suffocating. I leaned against the wall in the war room, my wounds aching with every shallow breath. Ruby was across from me, her hands still moving with practiced efficiency as she checked my bandages. The fact that she hadn't flinched when things had gone sideways earlier, when bullets had flown and chaos had erupted, spoke volumes about the woman I had at my side. She wasn't just my partner in this war. She was the reason we'd made it this far.

"You're pushing yourself too hard," Ruby said, her voice steady despite the stress etched on her features.

She was trying to hide it, but I saw the worry behind her eyes.

"I'll be fine," I muttered, trying to sound more convincing than I felt.

"Don't lie to me, Ryan. You've been shot multiple times in two nights. That's not something you just shake off." Her fingers tightened around the bandage she was adjusting on my side. "This is your fault too, you know. You always push yourself past the point of no return."

I looked down, letting out a short breath. She was right. I had done this to myself. But I wasn't about to let her shoulder this alone. Not now.

"What's next?" I asked, shifting the conversation. "We need to know what they're planning. The longer they wait, the worse it'll get."

Ruby paused, looking at me closely before responding. "We wait, Ryan. We don't go after them this time. We lure them in."
I felt a flicker of hesitation. We had been on the defensive for so long, I wasn't used to waiting. It felt wrong. But Ruby's plan had always had a way of working when nothing else made sense. I nodded, trying

to push aside the ache in my body and my mind. We had to wait, but that didn't mean we could relax. Every moment was another chance for them to strike.

The Gathering Storm

The hours stretched on as we continued our preparations. Mia and Leo were on the ground, setting up false leads to draw out Alessandro Vitale's men. Julie and Luca's forces were ready to reinforce us if needed, though we all knew it could be a trap. Every move was calculated. Ruby had taken the lead on the tactical operations, watching over the screens with a calm I didn't possess. She had an uncanny ability to read people, to anticipate their next steps. It was as though she knew what made them tick.

> "Leo's setting the traps for Vitale's people," she said, her eyes narrowing as she scanned the feed. "They won't see this coming."

I glanced over at her, pride swelling in my chest. The woman was a force of nature, even when we were backed into a corner. She had a sharpness to her that made every move count. We weren't just defending anymore. We were hunting. As the sun began to set, I felt the heavy weight of anticipation in my gut. Every movement, every noise, was amplified. We were about to enter another phase of this war, one where we could no longer afford to make mistakes.

The Trap is Set

Nightfall brought a strange stillness. As the hours passed, we monitored every signal, watching for any indication of movement. Ruby stood beside me, her sharp gaze never leaving the screens as we continued our vigil.

"Do you think this is the moment?" I asked, voice low.

Ruby didn't answer immediately. She was still studying the data in front of her, her eyes flicking from one screen to the next. Finally, she turned to me, her face set in grim determination.

"Yeah, I think it is. We've got one shot at this. If they take the bait, we move in. If not... we wait for them to slip up."

I rubbed a hand over my face, exhaustion hitting me harder now. Ruby was right. We had to be precise. Every move had to count. Then, the signal came.

"It's them," Mia's voice crackled through the comms. "They're moving. The trap's been sprung."

My heart rate spiked. "Let's do this."

The Final Stand

The moment we engaged, everything felt like it had slowed down. The tactical precision, the rehearsed movements, all came into play as we launched our counteroffensive. Luca's men were first into the fray, their weapons cutting through the night air as they took positions around the perimeter of Vitale's hideout.

I could hear the distinct sounds of gunfire in the distance, the shrill crack of bullets cutting through the quiet night. Inside, the tension was suffocating. But Ruby remained calm, her voice clear in my ear as she updated the team's positions.

"I need you to stay close," she said, her tone firm. "This isn't over. Stay sharp."

"I'm not going anywhere," I replied, my voice tight with the strain of the effort. "Not when we're this close."

We moved forward, our team advancing in synchronized formation. The noise of the battle intensified as we closed in on Vitale's stronghold. They were scrambling, reacting to the unexpected attack. We had them on the ropes. Then, it happened. A shot rang out from behind us, followed by the sound of multiple footsteps approaching quickly. Someone had broken through our defences. I barely had time to react before a bullet whizzed by, grazing my arm and leaving a fresh wound. My pulse quickened, and I could hear Ruby's voice, frantic and sharp.

"Ryan! Stay with me!"

But it wasn't the pain that was getting to me—it was the realization that our enemies had anticipated our every move. This wasn't over. Not by a long shot. The gunfire began to die down as we swept through the compound. The remaining enemy soldiers, once fierce in their resistance, now found themselves pushed into a corner. The battle had turned in our favour, and their chances of escape were slim. We had the upper hand. Luca's men and Mancini's remaining forces were everywhere, securing the perimeter and clearing rooms as Leo and Mia's team pressed forward. We weren't just fighting for our survival anymore. We were fighting for control, to show the world that the Sanguinetti family wasn't going anywhere.

The final blow came quickly. As we reached the last bastion of their resistance, the last of Vitale's men dropped their weapons, surrendering or falling under our fire. The fighting had become one-sided. I could barely feel the pain from my injuries anymore, but I still moved with purpose, knowing Ruby was behind me. She was by my side through it all, her presence both a constant and a reminder of everything we were fighting for. My gaze locked onto hers for a moment, and I could see the uncertainty still in her eyes. But I knew that she was with me—fully. And that was all that mattered. We moved toward the inner chambers of the compound. Inside, we found a high-ranking member of Vitale's inner circle, badly injured but still alive. His breathing was ragged, and blood stained his uniform. He looked up at me with recognition, fear flickering behind his gaze.

I moved to kneel beside him, my voice low and controlled. "Tell whoever's left—the D'Alessandro family, the remnants of Vitale's empire—that we—the Sanguinetti family—are here to stay. You've failed. This ends with us." The man coughed, wincing in pain, but his expression hardened. "You think you've won?" he rasped. "There's always someone willing to take our place..." I leaned in, my face close to his. "Then let them come. But know this: you'll never have the strength you had before. Not after what we've done here. Not after you've seen what we're capable of." I stood, looking down at him one last time before turning to Ruby. She was watching, standing strong despite the tension still crackling in the air. She knew what this moment meant. This was our stand, and no one—no one—was going to take this from us. The sound of gunfire had ceased, and our forces were securing the rest of the compound. The battle for control was ours, and there would be no more threats from Vitale or his men. They were gone.

But even as the dust began to settle, I knew the war wasn't over. This was just the beginning. We had won this battle. But the war, the fight for our future, was far from finished. And we would face it together. The Sanguinetti family, united once more.

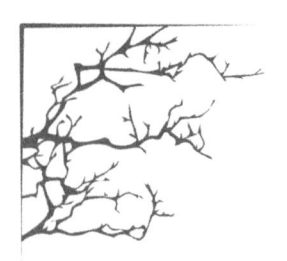

Crossroads

A month had passed since the battle that changed everything. The dust had settled, but the echoes of what we'd faced still lingered in the corners of our minds. The estate had returned to some semblance of normalcy, but I knew—Ruby knew—nothing would ever be the same again. We had taken down Alessandro Vitale, Francesca D'Alessandro, and the remnants of their forces. The battle for Horizon View was over. But the cost had been steep. In our pursuit of victory, we had lost people—friends, allies—and now, the weight of the choices we'd made was heavier than ever. I sat at my desk in the study, the sun setting beyond the estate's grounds, casting long shadows across the room. Ruby stood by the window, her arms crossed, looking out over the horizon.

"We're not done, are we?" she asked softly, her voice breaking the silence.

I didn't need to ask what she meant. The Famiglia Notturno was still out there. Despite everything we'd done, despite the lives we'd taken and the blood we'd spilled, their shadow still loomed over us. Our new name, the Sanguinetti family, was meant to be a fresh start—but it wasn't that simple. There were still debts to settle, and the Notturno family would make sure we paid them. I stood and joined her by the window, the night air cool as it brushed against my skin.

"No," I said, my voice low. "We're not done."

Ruby turned to face me, her gaze steady. "And what happens when the next battle comes? What happens when they come for us again?"

I met her eyes, and for a moment, the world outside faded away. She had been by my side through everything—through the bloodshed, the lies, the betrayals—and she deserved more than this. But I wasn't sure I could offer her a life free of danger, a life untouched by the consequences of the choices I'd made.

"I'll protect you," I said, my hand reaching for hers. "I'll protect all of us. I don't care what it takes."

Ruby squeezed my hand, but her expression remained conflicted. "At what cost, Ryan? How far are you willing to go? You've already lost so much. How much more can you sacrifice for revenge?" I looked away, unable to answer immediately. It was a question I had been asking myself for days. The Notturno family was still out there, still plotting. And I knew, deep down, that they wouldn't stop until they had destroyed everything we'd built. And yet, despite the toll it was taking on us, the fire for justice still burned. The hunger for vengeance had become part of me. It was a part of the past I had tried to bury but couldn't.

"We make our stand," I finally said, the decision settling in my chest like a weight I had to carry. "We end this now. We take control of our future. I won't let them destroy us."

Ruby stepped closer, her hand gently resting against my chest. "Then we'll do it together. But promise me, Ryan... promise me you won't lose yourself in this. We can fight, but we can't sacrifice everything." I closed my eyes for a moment, letting her words settle into me. "I promise."

But even as I said the words, I knew that this was just the beginning. The Famiglia Notturno wasn't done with us. And as much as I wanted to leave the past behind, it was clear now—my past was not done with me. The storm was far from over. The weight of the promise I made to Ruby felt both comforting and suffocating. She needed reassurance, but I wasn't sure I could give it to her completely. How could I promise not to lose myself in this fight when I wasn't entirely sure where I ended, and the battle began? The past had already taken so much from me, and it still had its hooks in deep. We stood there, locked in a silence that stretched between us like a taut wire. She was waiting for me to take the next step, and I could feel the tension in the air—both of us knowing that, despite all the words, the true test of our commitment to each other would come when the storm hit again. Finally, Ruby let out a soft sigh and turned her gaze back to the horizon. "I've been thinking about it, too. About what comes next. Not just for us, but for everyone who's been dragged into this... this war. It's not just about revenge anymore, is it?"

Her question lingered, and for a moment, I didn't know how to answer. The bloodshed, the planning, the manipulation—none of it felt like it was about anything pure anymore. It had become a relentless cycle, one that fed off itself. Every victory brought a new price, and the cycle turned again.

> "No," I said, my voice quieter now. "It stopped being about revenge a long time ago. But we can't turn back now. The Notturno family won't stop. And neither will I."

Ruby nodded slowly. "I know. And I'll stand with you. But I need to know, Ryan, that you're not doing this just to fight. That we're doing this to secure our future. For you. For me. For everyone who's still standing with us."

I felt a pang in my chest. I didn't deserve her unwavering support—not after all the lies I'd told, not after everything I'd kept from her. But as she stood there, strong and resolute, I saw something I hadn't realized before. She wasn't just asking for my promise to fight for her—she was asking for my promise to fight *with* her.

"I will, Ruby," I said, my voice firmer now. "We do this together. No more secrets, no more lies. From here on out, we take this fight on our terms."

She turned back to face me, her eyes full of determination. "Then let's make sure it counts." As I looked at her, I saw the resolve in her face—the same resolve that had brought us this far, through everything. We had been tested in ways most people could never understand, but it was clear now. The storm was coming, and we would face it side by side. I reached for her hand, pulling her closer, letting the warmth of her touch remind me of everything I was fighting for. I had already lost so much, but there was still so much more to protect. And Ruby? Ruby was everything. She was my reason to fight, my reason to survive. As we stood together, staring out at the estate below us, I knew we were standing on the edge of something bigger than either of us. There was no going back from this. The choices I made would either build a future or destroy it, but I couldn't live in the shadows any longer. The battle with the Famiglia Notturno wasn't over. But I wasn't afraid of the fight anymore. Because this time, we weren't fighting for survival alone.

We were fighting for *us*.

And that was a fight worth everything.

The next morning, the atmosphere was charged with the urgency of what was to come. We had already begun our preparations, consolidated our forces and called in allies who had been waiting in the wings. The time for hesitation was over. Ruby and I stood in the war room with Leo, Mia, and Julie, our trusted circle of people who had stuck by us, even when the odds had seemed insurmountable.

"This is it," Leo said, his voice steady. "We're not just taking the fight to the Notturno family anymore. We're going to end this. For good."

I nodded. "We must move fast. We know their strongholds, their connections. It's time to hit them where it hurts. We'll need everyone. Luca's people, Mancini's men—whoever we can rely on. But we need to make sure this is it. No more half-measures. No more waiting." Ruby, standing beside me, gave a determined nod. "I've been thinking about it, too. It's not just about bringing them down. It's about making sure there's nothing left for them to rebuild. We must burn the roots, not just cut the branches." Julie's voice cut through the room. "I've already put the word out. Luca's ready, and Mancini's men are on standby. But we need to act fast. Alessandro's men are already starting to regroup. We don't want to give them time to recover."

"We won't," I said, turning to face her. "We hit them fast. We hit them hard."

I could feel the weight of what was ahead, the responsibility to everyone in the room and everyone who had placed their trust in us. It wasn't just about me anymore. It was about us. About Ruby. About the future we were building together.

"Let's do this," I said.

With that, we moved into action.

The Notturno family thought they could break us. But they didn't know us. They didn't know *who* we had become.

We were no longer running from the shadows of our past. We were bringing the fight straight to them. And this time, there was no turning back.

We were going to take control of our future.

Once and for all. The air was thick with tension as we prepared to make our next move, but just before we took charge, a message came through from our prison cell guards.

"Mancini and Dante want a word," the voice on the comms said, the words heavy with an air of unexpected calm.

I turned to Ruby, who was standing close by, her face a mask of determination. She knew what this meant, just as well as I did. The men who had been once enemies, and then temporary allies, were now asking to speak. The next move wasn't going to be just about our fight against the Notturno family—it was about how we handled the people who had been part of our world for so long.

"They're getting bolder," I muttered under my breath, the thought lingering in my mind. Mancini was too smart to be left out of this game entirely, and Dante... well, Dante was always a wild card.

"We don't have time for games," Ruby replied, her voice firm. "But I know you'll do what needs to be done."

I gave a nod, and we made our way to the makeshift holding area where both Mancini and Dante were confined. We couldn't afford to show weakness, not now. Not when we had so much at stake. The shadows of the past were still there, but the light of our future had never been clearer.

Meeting Mancini

Mancini sat first, his posture stiff but respectful. His eyes gleamed with an intelligence that was sharp, calculating, and now, strangely, tinged with something like respect.

> "You've done it," Mancini said, his voice smooth but heavy with weight. "I thought you'd fail, like everyone before you, but you've done it. You've built something stronger than any of us could have imagined."

I didn't respond immediately, letting the silence stretch between us. His words were carefully chosen, and I could hear the underlying intent. Mancini wasn't just talking about us as if we were some fleeting forces, he was acknowledging our strength, the power we had reclaimed for ourselves.

"You're right about one thing," I said, my tone sharp. "We're stronger now. Stronger than you, and stronger than the Notturno family thought possible."

He didn't flinch at my words. Instead, he leaned forward, his gaze locked with mine. "I'm not foolish, Ryan. I see it now. I know where you're headed, and I know I'm not in your league anymore. But I've survived this long by knowing when to back the right horse. I'm asking you to let me stand with you now. My resources, my people—whatever you need." I exchanged a look with Ruby. Her expression was unreadable, but I could sense the hesitation in her body language. Mancini had been an adversary for so long, and his sudden offer of loyalty didn't sit well with her. But I knew what this moment meant. What *he* was offering.

"We'll consider it," I said, but my voice held the weight of finality. "You'll be watched. Betrayal won't be tolerated again. Stand with us, and you stand for the Sanguinetti family. You cross us, and you'll be dealt with, just like everyone else who's tried to bring us down."

Mancini gave a slight smile, the glint of a sharp calculation in his eyes. "Understood. I swear my loyalty to you, Ryan. To the Sanguinetti family." With that, we left him in his cell, the deal struck, but his every move from now on would be monitored. Trust wasn't something I could afford to give lightly, especially not after everything that had happened. But in this game, sometimes, allies were forged in strange ways.

Meeting Dante

The second meeting was far less cordial. Dante sat before me, his face cold, unreadable. He hadn't changed. The arrogance was still there, the smirk lingering like a permanent fixture.

"You really think I'm going to join you?" Dante scoffed, his voice dripping with contempt. "You think I'd betray my family for your pathetic little cause?"

Ruby stood at my side, her presence unwavering. There was no mistaking her disbelief in his words, the same disbelief I felt. Dante was nothing more than a power-hungry opportunist. He wasn't going to bend.

"You have a choice," I said, my voice a controlled force. "Stand with us, and I'll make sure you're protected. I'll make sure your men aren't thrown to the wolves. But if you choose to stand against us, then you'll answer for your actions."

Dante's eyes flickered for just a moment, doubt crossing his expression before the mask returned.

"I don't need your protection," he said, his voice cold. "I'll find my own way. I'll *never* stand with you."

Ruby's gaze never left him, and I could feel the tension between us. This was the last option. Dante had made his choice, and with it, he sealed his fate.

"You chose wrong," I said, my words deliberate and final. "The evidence we have against you is enough to bury you. You won't get another chance."

He opened his mouth to retort, but it was too late. We had already sent word to the authorities. The evidence we had gathered over the past weeks, including the damning proof of Peter's and Elena's deaths, was too overwhelming for him to escape. His dealings with the Notturno family, his countless crimes—they were all laid bare.

Dante was taken into police custody later that day. We'd given them everything they needed to make sure he was convicted. The trial was swift, the evidence irrefutable, and Dante was sentenced to life in prison. He would spend the remaining years of his life behind bars, alone, just as he had lived his life—isolated from everyone, even his own family. But, for us, this victory didn't feel like a win. It was a necessary step, a painful but essential part of securing our future. The family's grip on Horizon View was now tighter than ever, and as we took a breath, ready to move on to the next chapter, I knew that everything had changed. The Sanguinetti family was rising—stronger, fiercer, and determined to hold onto everything we'd fought for. And no one, not even those from our past, could take that away from us. The finality of Dante's fall settled over me, and for the first time in months, I allowed myself to breathe. But Ruby's grip on my hand was firm, her eyes meeting mine as she stepped closer.

"Is it over?" she asked, her voice quiet.

I shook my head, but this time, it wasn't from doubt. "No, Ruby. It's just the beginning." And with that, we stepped forward into a future of our making, where nothing and no one would threaten us again. A few days after Dante's arrest, the dust had settled, but the weight of what was still ahead hung heavy. The Sanguinetti family's power was intact, but the war wasn't over. Not yet. We had taken down Vitale, Francesca, and Dante, but the shadows of the past still loomed, and new enemies were already circling. We had to be ready for what was coming next. Mancini's release was the final piece in the puzzle, and though it was a move that many of my people viewed with scepticism, I knew we couldn't afford to keep enemies close who could have proven useful in the future. His loyalty was still untested, but now, it was a matter of leverage. He was back, and he was under our watchful eye.

He arrived at the estate's war room the following morning, looking every bit the calculating man I remembered. His presence was sharp, calculated, and just as dangerous as it had been when we first crossed paths. Ruby and I were seated at the table, and I could feel her tension beside me as Mancini entered, flanked by a couple of his men. His eyes scanned the room, assessing the power dynamics before he took a seat across from me.

"I don't take betrayal lightly," I said, my voice low, but carrying the weight of a promise. "But you're here now, and that's all that matters. For now."

Mancini gave a nod, but it wasn't just a nod of agreement—it was one of understanding. He knew the price of failure, and he knew the stakes of what he was about to get involved in.

"I didn't survive this long by being a fool," Mancini said, his tone calm but firm. "I've seen what you've done, Ryan. And I'm here now to ensure that I'm on the right side of history. I've got resources, intel, and men that can help you take down what's left of Vitale's network. If you'll have me."

Ruby's gaze flicked from Mancini to me, and I could sense the quiet war playing out in her mind. She wasn't thrilled about Mancini's presence, but I also knew that we needed every advantage we could get. She said nothing, but the unspoken agreement between us was clear. We couldn't afford to reject his help, not with the enemy forces still out there, regrouping. I leaned back in my chair, considering his offer. We had already lost too many men, fought too many battles. The last thing I wanted was to give Mancini the impression that I needed him more than he needed us. But the reality was that we needed him now—his expertise, his connections, and his ability to see through the fog of war.

"Alright," I said, breaking the silence. "But remember this, Mancini—if you cross us, there won't be a second chance."

His lips curved into a cold smile, the kind of smile that had made him a dangerous adversary for so long.

"Understood," Mancini replied. "I'm not here to play games. I'm here to win."

With that, he unfolded a set of maps and dossiers, sliding them across the table to me. The next phase of our plan was already taking shape. We had enemies to deal with, remnants of Vitale's influence that still held power in key areas. Mancini's resources would help us tighten our grip, and with his help, we could take back what was ours. Ruby squeezed my hand under the table, a silent promise that she would stand by me no matter what came next.

"Let's get to work," I said, looking around the room at those who had remained loyal to us.

Mancini's men, a few from Mancini himself, stood at the edges of the room, their eyes trained on us. We had all come to a crossroads. The next decisions would shape our future. But one thing was clear: no one, not Mancini, not the remnants of the Notturno family, or anyone else, could stop us now. We were The Sanguinetti. And we weren't backing down.

The planning began in earnest, with every detail mapped out, every move calculated. As Mancini settled into the war room, there was a shift in the air. This wasn't just a meeting of former enemies—it was the beginning of a new chapter in our battle. With him by our side, we would strike at the heart of what remained of Vitale's organization, and when it was done, we would control Horizon View and beyond. This war, though far from over, was one we could win. Together. And now, with our plan in place, we were ready to take the fight to them once and for all.

The countdown had begun.

The Price of Freedom

The walls of the war room were thick with tension, but this time, the weight on my shoulders was heavier than any battle we'd faced before. It wasn't just our enemies that I had to contend with—it was the remnants of a past I could never outrun. Ruby sat beside me, her hand resting on mine, offering a quiet but steadying presence. But even her unwavering support couldn't fully lift the storm cloud hanging over me. The shadows of the Notturno network loomed large, their influence still lingering over everything we had built. And now, with Vitale gone, there was nothing left standing in the way of our complete takeover—except the final vestiges of power, those who believed they could challenge us. Leo and Mia were finalizing the details of our next move when a comm came through, cutting through the low murmur of strategizing.

"We've got a situation," Leo said, his voice tight. "It's Mancini."

I looked up from the maps strewn across the table. "What now?"

"Mancini's making a move," Leo continued. "We've got eyes on him. He's not going to wait much longer. He knows the power shift is happening."

I exchanged a glance with Ruby. "Is he still loyal, or is this his play for power?"

"We'll find out soon enough," Leo replied.

As we sat in the tension-filled silence, I couldn't shake the nagging feeling that something bigger was brewing—something deeper. The Notturno network was like a beast with many heads, and just because

Vitale had fallen didn't mean the fight was over. Ruby's voice broke the stillness. "Ryan, we've come this far. Whatever comes next, we'll face it together." Her words hit me harder than any gunshot. As much as I knew the battles ahead could tear us apart, I couldn't imagine facing them without her.

"We need to take control, fully," I said, standing up. "This war isn't just about the fight; it's about the price we're willing to pay for freedom. We've already paid so much."

Mancini's loyalists had proven useful, but the question remained: would they stay loyal once the last of the Notturno network fell? Could we truly trust them? Before I could respond, the door to the war room opened. Mancini walked in, flanked by his men, a slight but noticeable tension between them and the rest of our team. His eyes flickered between Ruby and me, a silent acknowledgment of the uneasy truce we'd struck.

"I've been watching you," Mancini said, his gravelly voice steady. "You've done what most of us only dreamed of. The Notturno network is falling. Vitale is dead, and the rest will crumble."

He paused, taking a long breath. "I've made my choice. My loyalty is with you now. But I need your help. There's no going back." I studied him, the weight of his words settling heavily. His history was filled with backstabbing and betrayal, but there was no denying his value now. The question remained: could I trust him?

"Mancini," I said, finally breaking the silence. "You know what's at stake. We're fighting for more than just survival. We're fighting to own this future."

He nodded, grimacing. "I'm not asking for mercy. Just the chance to fight beside you." Ruby stepped forward, her eyes hard. "This is your one shot. Prove your loyalty, and it's yours. Cross us, and you'll wish you never had the chance." Mancini looked at her, a flicker of respect in his eyes. "Understood." I gestured to the table, where maps and intelligence reports lay open. "Then let's get to work. We end this, once and for all." As Mancini settled in at the table, the final pieces of our strategy began to come together. This wasn't just about winning a battle; it was about securing our future. The road ahead would be fraught with peril, but we were ready. And when the time came, we would be ready to take back what was ours—no matter the cost. The war room was still, save for the sound of the occasional marker scribbling on a map or the tapping of fingers on the table. Everyone was on edge, fully aware that this would be a defining moment in our fight. Mancini sat quietly across from me, his face as hard and unreadable as ever. Yet, his posture wasn't that of a man claiming dominance—it was one of a man trying to prove his worth.

Ruby stood beside me, her hand still resting lightly on my arm, as if reminding me she was here—through everything. The weight of her support was immeasurable, yet the questions between us remained unspoken. Trust was fragile, and we both knew it. But we couldn't afford to let that break us now.

"What's the plan?" Mancini's voice cut through the silence, his eyes sharp, alert.

His willingness to get involved wasn't surprising, but the speed with which he'd aligned himself with us was. That had to mean something. I looked at the team gathered around the table—Leo, Mia, Luca, our men, and what remained of Mancini's loyalists. Everyone was waiting for the next move, every face reflecting the same hard resolve I felt inside.

"We strike tonight," I said, my voice low but firm. "We've taken the Notturno network's head off, but their influence still lingers. We need to send a message. Once and for all. We take control of the last stronghold they hold over Horizon View, and we eliminate the remaining threats."

Ruby's eyes met mine, a silent question passing between us. The final blow to the empire we had been born into—the one that had haunted us for years—was now within reach. But it wasn't just the end of a legacy—it was the end of an era. I nodded. "This is it. We finish what we started." The room was silent for a beat, then Leo spoke. "We'll need more firepower to take them down for good. If we're going to push Vitale's old men out, we need to hit hard and fast." Mancini chimed in, "I've got men waiting outside the perimeter. We can move quickly, silently. You'll get your chance." Mia stepped forward, her eyes scanning the intelligence reports laid out on the table. "We've been tracking their movements for days. We know where they're most vulnerable. If we move now, they won't have time to regroup."

Ruby's voice interrupted the planning, strong and unwavering. "Ryan, you know what this means. There's no turning back after this. If we do this, we're not just killing a network—we're becoming the target for whatever remains of the Famiglia Notturno. Everyone who's ever known us will come for us." I met her gaze, seeing the hesitation, the doubt in her eyes. I understood it, but this was no longer a question of what was right—it was about survival. It was about our future.

"I'm ready," I said, my voice a bit too firm, though the weight of the decision pressed down on me harder than I let on.

Ruby's gaze softened, but there was still a trace of uncertainty in her eyes. "I'm with you, no matter what. But remember, Ryan, we can't do this alone. You've already lost so much. We can't lose each other." Her words were a soft plea, wrapped in the steel of determination. I squeezed her hand gently, understanding that this battle wasn't just against our enemies—it was against the ghosts of the past that threatened to tear us apart.

"We won't," I assured her, my voice low but resolute. "We're taking this fight together. But we need to be smart."

I turned back to the table. "Here's the plan—tonight, we strike. The rest of you will secure the perimeter, ready to move at a moment's notice. Luca, I want you to take your men and focus on the outer buildings. Clear them out first. Mia, Leo, we'll handle the main building. Make sure Mancini's men stay out of our way." Mancini nodded, his eyes cold, calculating. "We'll do our part." I looked at the map, the familiar tension settling into my chest. Every decision from here on out would either lead us to victory or expose us to the final wave of the storm we'd been fighting. Ruby leaned over, her voice barely above a whisper. "Promise me this won't destroy us." I met her gaze, my heart clenching at the thought. "I promise."

A Quite reflection

The hours leading up to the assault passed in a blur. Each step felt like we were walking the razor's edge, where one wrong move could mean the end. The air in the safe house grew thick with anticipation, but none of us allowed the fear to show.

We were ready.

The final showdown was upon us.

The last of Vitale's remnants

The team split off, our movements deliberate, precise. The men who had joined us—Mancini's, Luca's, and what was left of our own—moved with one singular purpose. There was no turning back. We hit their compound hard, with the full force of everything we had built. A heavy barrage of gunfire echoed in the distance as we took the first set of buildings, clearing them with swift, brutal efficiency.

Mancini's men followed our lead, as if they had been part of our group from the start. But we both knew that loyalty wasn't something you could buy with power—it was something you earned. And the night was far from over. I led the charge into the main building, the dark halls eerily quiet as we moved through them. Every corner was a potential trap, every shadow a threat.

Then came the explosion. It was sudden, deafening. The building shook beneath us, dust and debris falling from the ceiling. But there was no time to stop. We pushed forward, knowing that if we let up for even a second, we could lose it all. We hit their strongest point—the nerve centre—hard, and within moments, the battle was ours. The sound of heavy gunfire filled the air, mingled with the occasional shout of victory. But it wasn't over. I moved through the smoke and the chaos, my focus sharp, my mission clear. We needed to break them down completely, and we would. And when the smoke cleared, we stood victorious, but we knew the cost had been high. With the last of the enemy forces neutralized, I made my way to the centre of the compound. There, standing in the rubble, was the man I had come to see. Mancini, standing tall and resolute beside Infront of me, met my gaze with a sharp nod.

> "We've won," I said, my voice heavy with the weight of the night's battle.

And for the first time in a long while, I allowed myself to believe it was true. The air was thick with the aftermath of the battle—exhausted bodies, the scent of smoke still lingering in the air, and the heavy weight of what had just transpired. We'd successfully eliminated Vitale's network, but the shadows of the Notturno were still looming over us. We weren't finished. The Notturno was still out there, and if they were breathing, our work was far from over.

"What's next, Ryan?" she asked softly, the question hanging between us.

I could feel the weight of it, the uncertainty in her voice. Even after everything we had fought for, there was still the question of what came after the fight. What would we become when it was all over? I looked at her, my chest tightening at the thought. She'd been with me through everything—the betrayals, the lies, the bloodshed—but this? This was different. The Notturno had always been the shadow over everything we built, the ghost of my past. Until that was gone, we could never truly be free.

"We end the Notturno," I said, my voice low but firm. "We take them out completely. It's the only way we can move forward."

Ruby met my gaze, her eyes flickering with something unreadable. I couldn't tell if she was questioning me or simply trying to make sense of everything. But I knew, deep down, this wasn't just about me. It was about us. The choices I made—what I did and who I was—affected more than just the man standing before her.

The door to the war room opened, and Mancini stepped inside, flanked by two of his men. His expression was grim, but there was something else there too—respect, maybe even a hint of understanding.

"Ryan," Mancini began, his voice steady. "We've finished with the Vitale network. You've earned my loyalty. I'll help you finish the job."

I studied him for a moment, the words weighing heavily in the air. There was no way around it—Mancini's assistance would be invaluable. We'd fought hard to get where we were, and now, with his help, we had a real shot at taking the Notturno down for good. But I knew better than to trust easily. Loyalty was a fragile thing.

"You've got one chance, Mancini," I said, my voice cold.

Mancini nodded, unflinching. "I understand. We're on the same side now." Ruby didn't say anything as she watched the exchange, but I could feel her eyes on me. She was wary of Mancini, of his intentions, but there was no time to question alliances now. If he was willing to fight with us, then we had to take advantage of it. Mancini's men took their positions around the room, and the strategy began to take shape.

Preparation for final battle

A few hours later, we gathered in the war room, the next steps clear in front of us. Mancini had given us information about the remaining factions of the Notturno network, but we couldn't afford to let our guard down. The next phase of the battle was going to be even more dangerous than the last.

> "We hit them hard," I said, my voice a low growl. "We take their strongholds. No mercy. The Notturno won't get another chance to strike at us."

Ruby stood beside me, her gaze unwavering. I could feel the weight of her silent support, but I knew she was still grappling with the choices I had made, with the cost of what we were doing. She placed a hand on my arm, a silent plea for me to consider the bigger picture. "Just don't lose yourself in this, Ryan. We can't keep going down this road if it means losing everything we've fought for." I turned to her, my eyes softening. "I won't lose us, Ruby. I swear."

The fall of The Notturno

Mancini's men were already gearing up, ready to help us take the fight to the Notturno. Leo and Mia had their team in place, and the plan was set. There was no turning back now.

"We move out at dawn," I said. "This ends now. For good."

As we prepared for the final battle, I knew that the road ahead was going to be even more dangerous. But we had come this far, and we wouldn't stop until the Notturno was nothing more than a ghost of the past. The final stand was approaching, and this time, there would be no turning back. We hit the last compound with all that we had and with tremendous precision. An all-out battle for peace, for freedom. We took the storm to The Notturno...The compound was eerily silent as we stood victorious. The air was heavy with the weight of what had just transpired—the final battle, the crushing losses, and the moments we'd never get back. The echoes of the gunfire had barely settled, but a strange calm began to settle over the battlefield. The enemy had fallen. And we were still standing.

Judie arrived, her steps measured and purposeful, though there was something in her eyes—a flicker of something deeper, something darker, that I couldn't ignore. She came to assess the final victory, to make sure the dust had truly settled. But I couldn't shake the feeling that this victory wasn't as complete as it seemed. The weight of it all, the years of fighting, still hung on my shoulders. But before we could even catch our breath, I saw her. Through the window of the compound, a figure moved, a woman with fiery red hair, sharp and striking, standing perfectly still. She wasn't someone I recognized, but there was something in her expression that caught my attention—a smile, dark and knowing, something that sent a shiver down my spine. My instincts screamed at me. Something wasn't right.

Without warning, two shots rang out from the roof. One of the bullets hit Mancini, sending him crashing to the ground taking his life instantly, and the other struck Judie. I heard the sharp intake of her breath, the gasp of pain, as she fell to the ground. The world seemed to slow as I rushed to her side.

"Mom!" I shouted, dropping to my knees beside her.

Her face was pale, her body trembling, but there was a strength in her eyes that told me she wasn't finished yet. Not yet. She gasped for breath, her voice coming out strained, each word a battle. "Finish this, Ryan... I love you... my precious boy..." And then, with one final, shuddering breath, the light left her eyes. The matriarch of our family. Gone. I gritted my teeth, a wave of anger washing over me, but there was no time to mourn. The fight wasn't over yet. Leo and Luca were already on the move, taking out the snipers who had fired from the roof, but my focus was still on Judie. She was gone, but the woman who had caused it all—the one standing in the window—was still out there.

Ruby looked at me, her gaze steady and resolute. Without words, she knew what needed to be done. We couldn't wait any longer. We had to end this now. Together, we rushed inside, making our way through the compound toward the source of the threat. Every corner seemed to hold a danger, every shadow hiding something we couldn't see. But we kept pushing forward, driven by the same resolve that had kept us alive all this time. We reached the top floor of the compound, the last stronghold of the Notturno's operations. The door to the room was slightly ajar, and I could feel her presence before I even saw her—waiting. Watching. When I pushed the door open, I saw her by the window, standing, waiting.

> "So, we meet at last, Roy Giovannetti," she said, her voice cold, her smile twisted in a way that made my skin crawl.

I froze at the sound of my name. Roy. Only my father ever called me that. It was a reminder of everything I had tried to leave behind. Of the family I had walked away from, only to have it haunt me at every turn. I stood tall, the anger rising in me. "Who are you?" I asked, my voice steady despite the fury I felt building inside me. Her smile deepened, the darkness in her eyes growing. "I'm Dom's daughter, Christina Giovannetti" she said, her words like a cold slap. "From an affair he had years ago. You didn't know about me, did you? He brought me into the Notturno when he knew his time was running out. He needed someone to continue his work after you abandoned it. I ran the shadows while you ran from the family." The weight of her words hit me like a freight train. She had been the one pulling the strings all along, the one who had been behind every attack, every scheme designed to destroy us. And she was right. My father had known his time was short. He had made sure his empire would continue—through her.

She sneered at me, her eyes cold. "You've killed our father, your family, everything you once were. And now, I'm here to avenge him." Her words hung in the air, bitter and final. But I wasn't done yet. I would not let her win. Not after everything we had sacrificed. Without warning, she drew a sidearm, aiming it directly at me, her hand steady and sure. But before she could pull the trigger, a gunshot rang out, the sound echoing in the room. Christina staggered back, her face frozen in shock. The bullet had missed me, but it didn't miss her.

Ruby stood behind me, her gun still raised. The shot had been perfect. One clean hit. Christina dropped to the floor, her weapon slipping from her hand. I stood there in shock, the weight of the moment settling over me. The final member of the Notturno's bloodline was gone. Christina Giovannetti, the last of my father's legacy, had fallen. And with her, the Notturno's shadow was finally gone. Ruby stepped forward, her gun lowered, her expression unreadable. She locked eyes with me, her gaze filled with something I couldn't quite place. But I knew one thing—it was over.

We had done it. We had survived.

As I looked down at Christina's lifeless body, the reality of it hit me hard. The war that had consumed our lives for so long was over. The Notturno was finished.

We could finally rebuild. Together.

The weight of everything we'd endured, all the pain, the loss, the betrayal—it was all behind us now.

We had won.

And as I turned to Ruby, I knew that we had finally earned the future we had fought so hard for.

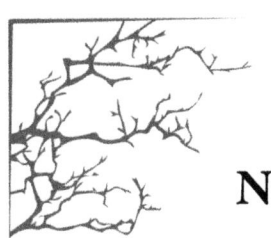

Next in the series!

*G*ardens of Resilience awaits: "In the quiet aftermath of victory, Ryan and Ruby face the delicate task of rebuilding not just their lives but the very foundation of their future. With new responsibilities, old scars, and the lingering shadows of past enemies, they must navigate the treacherous road of healing and reconciliation. As they extend their hands to help the community of Horizon View, a new set of challenges threatens to undo everything they've fought for—both in the world they seek to protect and in the fragile bonds they've forged with each other."

Don't miss out!

Visit the website below and you can sign up to receive emails whenever R. Stellan publishes a new book. There's no charge and no obligation.

https://books2read.com/r/B-A-VPMVC-FOQIF

BOOKS2READ

Connecting independent readers to independent writers.

Did you love *Veins of Vengance*? Then you should read *The Blood Pact*[1] by R. Stellan!

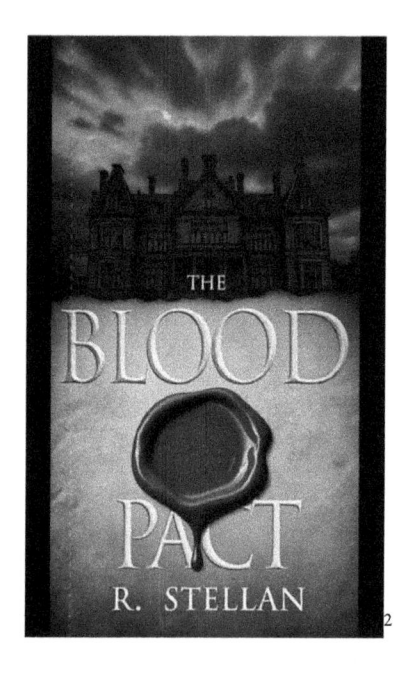

Giovannetti has spent his life running from the dark legacy of the notorious Notturno family—a powerful criminal empire bound by blood and ruthless loyalty. Haunted by secrets and pursued by enemies from his past, Ryan walks a dangerous tightrope, desperate to escape the shadows that threaten to consume him. Ruby Smith is a fiercely independent woman with a haunted past of her own. Determined to build a better future, she crosses paths with Ryan at a pivotal moment, drawn to the enigmatic man despite the danger that follows him. Together, they form a reluctant alliance, bound by mutual need and an undeniable connection that neither expected. As threats close in from all sides, Ryan and Ruby must navigate a world where betrayal is

---

1. https://books2read.com/u/3Gq7oO

2. https://books2read.com/u/3Gq7oO

inevitable, trust is a gamble, and survival comes at a steep cost. Facing relentless enemies and impossible choices, their bond deepens into something neither of them dared hope for: love. But when loyalty and love are tested in the ultimate crucible, will their pact be strong enough to protect them from the dark forces closing in?

The Blood Pact is the first thrilling instalment of the *Notturno Affair* series—a story of love forged in adversity, courage tested in the face of danger, and the fight to break free from the chains of the past.

Read more at https://rstellan24.my.canva.site/.

Also by R. Stellan

The Notturno Affair
The Blood Pact
Veins of Vengance

Watch for more at https://rstellan24.my.canva.site/.